The Night's Baby:

A Black Vampire Story

The Night's Baby:

A Black Vampire Story

Stina

URBAN
Renaissance

www.urbanbooks.net

Urban Books, LLC
300 Farmingdale Road, NY-Route 109
Farmingdale, NY 11735

The Night's Baby: A Black Vampire Story
© 2019 Stina

ISBN 13: 978-1-60162-908-1
ISBN 10: 1-60162-908-7

First Mass Market Printing May 2019
First Trade Paperback Printing March 2018
Printed in the United States of America

10 9 8 7 6 5 4 3 2 1

*This is a work of fiction. Any references or similarities
to actual events, real people, living or dead, or to real
locales are intended to give the novel a sense of reality. Any similarity in other names, characters, places,
and incidents is entirely coincidental.*

Distributed by Kensington Publishing Corp.
Submit Orders to:
Customer Service
400 Hahn Road
Westminster, MD 21157-4627
Phone: 1-800-733-3000
Fax: 1-800-659-2436

The Night's Baby:

A Black Vampire Story

by

Stina

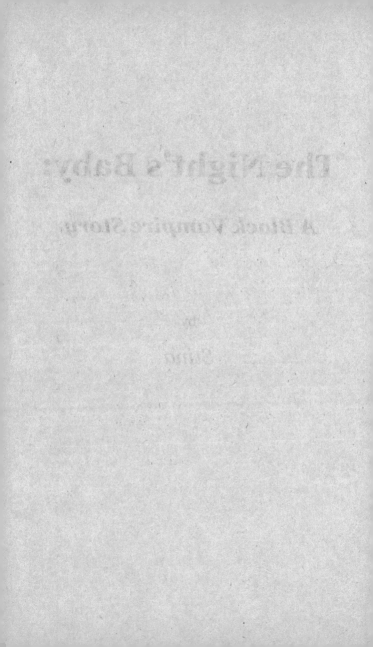

Prologue

"The great war is approaching, I can feel it. If our mortal enemy senses our divide, then this could be the end of all vampire life. What are we to do?"

The room was silent as the vampires sitting at the round table pondered over their next words. The dining room of the vast mansion was dimly lit, being as the only light came from each candle the eight had in front of them. It had been centuries since they were all together, but times had called for the Ancients to come together as one. There was a shift in the balance of the underworld, and they all felt it. It was unsettling, and they all harbored something that had been distant from their hearts for so long: fear.

"Tep, do not be so dramatic," a woman finally spoke up. She leaned forward so that the smooth chocolate skin on her timeless face could be seen. Her long dreads were pinned back neatly in a bun and her amber eyes pierced into the others who were present. Her full lips were dark red, as if she had just gotten done feeding on mortal blood, and her high cheekbones accented her gorgeous face. She looked around the room and then rested her eyes on Tep, the vampire who'd spoken first.

His hair was cut short and, although he was three centuries old, he didn't look to be a day over twenty-five. His smooth caramel skin glowed in the minimal light, and his brown eyes spoke to her even when his lips didn't. He was weary; they all were. Not only did it seem that the new-age vampires had completely forgotten their way but, with their divide, only weakness showed.

"Please explain to me how I am being dramatic. The Malum and Sefu have been at war for far too long. They cannot even sense the real evil coming. We have not had to show our faces for years, Dena. No one is supposed to know of our existence. Not since Adie . . ."

Tep's voice trailed off, but everyone knew what he was talking about. The Ancients consisted of Tep, Dena, Brax, Lira, Xion, Rain, Eron, and Constance. They were among the first vampires known to man, being as they were all created by Dracula himself. When he turned them all, he gave them all a different special gift along with immortality. Although Dracula hadn't been seen or heard of since their makings, they remained. There was once a ninth Ancient, Adie, who died in a great battle. However, right before she died, she placed her essence inside of a new vampire, giving him the power of the Ancients. He, known to those around him as Kesh, was the king of the Sefu clan. To his knowledge, he was the oldest of the vampires, and for a while, that was how the Ancients preferred to keep it. When Adie turned him, he was deemed untouchable due to it being unlawful for a vampire to kill another vampire. They, however, did keep a close watch on him in hopes that he would be the one to unite all vampires.

"Kesh has failed to do his duty as king." The deep voice of Xion, a muscular vampire, sounded. The brow on his vanilla-chocolate face furrowed and it was evident that he could not hide his displeasure. "In his rule, not only were more vampires created unlawfully, but a new clan emerged with a king with nothing but vengeance in his heart. Vampires against vampires? This has been unheard of!"

"I know, Xion, but—"

"But nothing, Dena. We are all at risk. It has been a year that we have waited, yet still, nothing has changed. We need to eliminate the threat and front line the great war ourselves!"

"You know we cannot do that!" Lira argued. Although her skin was mahogany brown, her hair was so gray that it looked silver. "Even with all of our strength combined, it will still not be enough. We need soldiers."

"Lira is right! We cannot battle our enemies without an army. It would be suicide. We must let Kesh do what he is meant to do. It's what Adie would have wanted."

"Dena," Tep began in a firm voice, "I understand that Adie was your sister, but it is time to do what we must do. He is the reason for the divide. It is an army that you want? The only way to unite all of the vampires is to get rid of one common factor. We must eliminate Kesh and his family."

"You will not lay a hand on them!" Dena's voice changed from smooth to deep and menacing at Tep's suggestion. She snarled and brandished her fangs. "Kesh is the only vampire Adie ever made. His woman is a direct descendant of Adie, which means the blood that courses through their veins is Adie's blood. My blood. I will rip your throats out if any of you harm a hair on their heads."

"But their child—" Eron started.

"Their child?" Dena cut him off. "Their child is the first-ever born vampire Ancient. That alone is enough reason to protect them with our lives." She cut her eyes at the seven sitting around her, taking in the uncertainty in their expressions. If she could slap each and every one of them with fierce force, she would.

"Also, Tep," she continued, "you are wrong. Just as the other vampires are wrong. The key to reproduction does not lie in Kesh's blood; it lies in Adirah's. In Adie's. That was her gift. The gift of reproduction. It is something that cannot be given or taken. The others cannot drink from her and obtain that gift; you have to be a direct blood relative. This is the reason Adirah has the gift to see spirits and the same reason that, when the time comes, her son will have that special gift too. Now do you understand that although Kesh was turned by Adie, he was not able to reproduce until now?"

There was quiet around the room until Constance, a petite vampire woman, gave Dena a knowing look. "How long have you been following her?"

"The same length of time I followed her mother, and her grandfather: her entire life. It wasn't until now that a gift finally awakened in one of my sister's offspring. I will guard Adirah and her son with my life."

Constance nodded and then turned back to the others. "It is settled then. We will find Kesh and his family, and we will begin to prepare them for war."

Chapter 1

There was a loud thud as her feet hit the ground. Usually, she trained with her clan, but that day Calum needed to do it alone. Lately, her mind had been clouded, not with vengeance, but with disappointment. She was disappointed in herself. How could she have been defeated that easily? She was beaten by a mortal. Well, at the time, she was mortal. Stories in the wind had come back and told her that Adirah was now a turned vampire, which meant that she was even stronger than before. Calum knew that in order to beat her in battle she would have to train ten times as hard.

The Malums' new home was a treat for the eyes. It had once belonged to a very wealthy man in Maryland before Talum turned him. Desperate times called for desperate measures and after the last battle everything, including their wealth, had been depleted. The man, Thomas Langstan, was the owner of a Fortune

500 tech company called Flago, a company in which Talum now had joint shares. The mansion was built on its own land in a forested area, and their neighbors were a good thirty-minute drive away. It was the perfect place for the Malum clan to recuperate and come back better and stronger than ever. The mansion had four floors. The basement had been completely redone and turned into sleeping quarters for them. Calum's and Talum's coffins, however, were of course in the master bedroom, a room that Thomas so graciously offered to his new king and queen.

The surrounding land had been turned into a training ground, and right then Calum was taking full advantage of it. Her senses heightened, and she sniffed the air before moving quickly to the side.

Pfft! Pfft! Pfft!

She'd moved just in time because the place where she was just standing was riddled with sharp stakes. Her bionic senses kicked in, and she heard the automatic machine that spat the stakes wind up again in the distance. It had a motion sensor and, no matter where she went, it would find her. Her training objective was to get to the off switch. The only thing was the machine was far, and there would be many obstacles in her way trying to stop her.

"Go!" she said to herself.

The knowledge that the training course would cause real pain added enough fuel to her fire. She took a breath and ascended toward her target. The wind flapped her long, straight hair and the trees around her blurred.

Boom!

It sounded as if a rocket had been let off. It wasn't a rocket, but the boulder being launched full force her way might as well have been.

"Ahh!"

Her battle cry sounded as she launched herself up in the air and used her right fist to punch the thick rock. Her hand didn't go right through it like she wanted it to, but it did some damage. The boulder flew the other way, and she landed gracefully, ducking at the exact moment that another was thrown at her. She knew that, as long as she was standing in that spot on the simulation course, the rocks would not stop coming. Her body was agile as she fought her way through until, finally, she reached a clearing.

It was quiet, too quiet. The thing about the simulation course was that every time it was turned on, the courses would be different. Calum didn't know what was next because last time the boulders were last. The hairs on the back of her neck stood up, and she sensed that she was not alone. Something, or someone, was circling her, stalking her, and trying to get a feel for her movements. She sniffed the air to get a whiff of whatever it was, and her eyes got bigger.

Snap!

Before she could prepare herself, a full-grown tiger presented itself by leaping out on top of her. She used her strength to hold its snarling mouth from taking off a chunk of her face. The look in the tiger's eyes was all too familiar to her.

Hunger.

She knew the tiger would do anything in its power to make her its prey. She was so busy keeping its mouth from inching closer to her that she forgot about its claws.

"Ah!" she cried in pain as she felt the claws swipe across her belly. The leather of her one-piece jumpsuit ripped easily, and so did her skin. She smelled her own blood and so did the tiger, because it bucked harder.

"Not today!"

Calum ignored the searing pain on her torso and gathered all her power to send the tiger flying to the side. She got to her feet and allowed herself to transform. She felt her muscles grow slightly and she brandished her fangs. The nails on her hands grew to weapons so sharp they could cut through the thickest of glass. She hissed at the tiger as she crouched into a battle position.

In front of her, the tiger changed to where it was no longer a tiger. She saw Adirah in front of her, and her heart rate quickened. There was no way she would allow her enemy to leave that place with a breath in her body. At the same time, the two launched full speed toward each other and crashed violently together. Neither one stumbled or backed down. Calum's arms moved with skill and speed as she landed each and every attack until, finally, she had taken the advantage.

She had Adirah pinned down on the grassy plane, looking frail and helpless with several gashes in her body. The vein on her neck was exposed, and suddenly Calum remembered her wound. Without another thought, she clamped down on her victim's throat and fed until she could no longer hear or feel a heartbeat. By the time she was done, the deep cuts on her stomach were completely healed, and it was like there was never anything there in the first place. Her entire face was covered in blood when she stood up. She smiled looking down at the dead tiger, pleased. She knew then how hard she would fight when she finally did see Adirah.

She heard a tiny whistle in the air, as if something was coming her way. Without turning around or moving, she put one hand up and caught in midair the stake going at least one hundred miles per hour. She'd grown tired of the course and was ready to end it, not complete it.

She grunted loudly as she spun and threw the long, thick wooden stake in the direction of the automatic weapon launching the deadly things her way in the first place. It took all of five seconds for her to hear the stake connect, followed by a big crash. She dusted her hands together, satisfied with herself, and made to go back to the mansion.

"That's the third one you've broken in the past month. At first, I thought it was accidental. Now I see there was always a purpose."

Calum looked up and smirked at the sight of her king. He'd stepped out from behind a tree in the distance. He too was wearing black fighting gear. His hair was newly cut, and he looked more handsome than ever. In a perfect world the two of them would have grown old together and had as many children as they could stand, but life had different plans for them. She was just happy that during her eternal hell she had someone who loved her as much as she did him to walk the path with her.

"You've gotten better at hiding your scent," Calum told him, "even from me. How long have you been watching?"

"For hours. You fight with such diligence these days."

"We cannot be defeated again, my love. We underestimated our enemies last time. That will never happen again. I almost lost you, and you me. That thought haunts my dreams every night. The Sefu must pay for these nightmares."

Talum nodded and walked to where Calum was standing. The normally smooth cocoa skin around her mouth was still covered in blood, and her jet-black hair was badly disheveled. Still, he felt that there was no other as beautiful as his queen. He admired her for her drive. She was strong and could endure much pain. Like him, however, she could not take with defeat what came along. She was a strong vampire, the strongest female vamp he'd ever met. That was, until he saw what Adirah could do. He knew that was eating Calum alive inside, and that was why he made it his job to push her harder than she would push herself.

"How did you get a tiger into these lands?"

Talum could not help but smile at her question. She was so smart, never letting anything slip past her. "Thanks to our new recruit and business venture, we have enough money to do whatever we want."

"How long did you starve it before deciding to use it in my training?"

"One week. Enough so that it would be hungrier than it had ever been, but not so hungry that it would be weak."

Calum's eyes went back to the dead beast, and she nodded in understanding. "Thank you, my king," she said and took his hand in hers. She sucked the blood from her teeth and made a face. "Next time, make it a bear. I don't think I'm too fond of tiger blood."

"Anything for you, my queen."

"Any news on the Sefu?"

As they walked through the forest and back to their home, Talum read between the lines of her question. "They are still in hiding, and that means that their king has not yet returned to them."

"And our spy?"

"He has no news of the Sefu."

"Then what use is he to us? Hasn't he served his purpose?"

"No, he has not." Talum kissed her hand. "Remember, he was the closest to Kesh. He knows him in ways that we never will. And now, he has the same distaste for his old king as I did when I first set off on my own. When the time comes, he will help me to destroy the Sefu once and for all."

"How can you be so sure?"

"Vampires like Tiev are powerful, but he is not a king. He seeks the protection of an umbrella. We will be that umbrella. Until he gives us what we want."

"Watch him."

"Ahh," he said with a chuckle, "my vigilant Calum. We will not let him out of our sight."

"And the baby?"

There seemed to be a shift in the air around them at the mention of Kesh and Adirah's offspring. It was no secret that the entire vampire world, including the Sefu, felt a certain way about the fact that Kesh had had a child. They felt that the secret to reproduction was in his blood and, at first, Talum felt the same way. But the more he thought about it, the more he ruled that out. He, himself, had been turned by Kesh not only by a bite. He had actually drunk from Kesh's blood, which meant he too had the same blood coursing through him. But he had not been able to reproduce, which meant that the key to having children did not lie in Kesh. It lay in Adirah. It had to. She was different, and she held the powers of vampires before she was even fully turned. He didn't know what it was, but there was something special about her.

These were speculations that he often kept to himself, simply because he did not want to give Calum another reason to have hatred in her heart. He hated to see her on edge the way she had been. Although he was the one who started the war, he was beginning to tire of the destruction caused by it. By becoming a king, he had vowed to protect his clan; instead, he kept leading them down paths of destruction. And that was why when he found Kesh and his family, he vowed to make their deaths as quick as possible, and never go to war with another as long as he lived.

Chapter 2

"This boy is a handful." Adirah sat in the kitchen of their quaint home and stared, admiring her perfect little boy. The kinky curls all over his head, mixed with his dimples and wide, light brown eyes, made him the cutest little boy she'd ever seen. He was the perfect mixture of herself and Kesh, but he definitely had her eyes. They were the same eyes she shared with her mother.

He sat happily in his high chair clapping his hands and eating his baby food. Adis was the first of his kind: a day walker. He could still live off of regular food and go out in the sun without a special ring. However, he had a strength not normal of a baby, and he was developing faster. He learned how to walk when he was only eight months old, and he had a thirst for blood. That was the reason they were not able to take him out around animals; he would kill them and drink from them. Kesh told Adirah that it was something he would grow out of, because for him it was not something he would ever need unless he was weak. It was like an energy booster, because he would grow to be stronger than all of them without the need for blood.

"Just like his father already." Kesh came from behind her with a grin.

At the sight of Kesh, Adis began to clap his hands harder and bounce in his chair. Kesh leaned down and kissed his little forehead before standing straight again and kissing Adirah's lips.

"What's for dinner?" Kesh joked and headed to the fridge that they kept in the garage.

When he returned with two fresh pouches of blood, he noticed that Adirah had taken Adis out of his high chair and gotten him all cleaned up already. She was making funny faces at him and making him giggle from deep in his belly. The love she held in her eyes for their son was so pure. She was barefoot and dressed casually in a baby blue blouse and a pair of jeans that hugged her newfound curves. She had a glow: not the vampire glow, but a different kind of glow that only motherhood could bring.

"Motherhood suits you," Kesh said, setting the two pouches of blood on the tall, square kitchen table.

"Thank you, honey," she said as she rocked Adis and listened to his coos. She could tell that he was sleepy by the way that he kept blinking his eyes and fidgeting in her arms. She knew that after a nice warm bath he would be knocked out. "I'm about to go and get him ready for bed. When I come back, we can pretend we're trying to make another."

She winked sexily at Kesh and made her way to the back of the one-story house. The house was a step up from what she was used to growing up, but she knew that it was something that Kesh had to get used to. The only good thing was that their backyard had a pond and many trees. Also, all of their neighbors were older folks who didn't care to poke their noses in their business. Adirah tried to make their new normal life as seamless as possible, especially for Kesh. He was a king subjected to living like a peasant temporarily. She didn't know how much longer they would have to live like that, but for the time being, she figured it was the safest thing for them.

With both the Malum and the Sefu clans at odds with them, she knew they couldn't resurface until they were absolutely ready. Although she had defeated Calum, she was not battle ready. When she got involved with Kesh, she never really thought about what the title of being his queen would really entail. It wasn't like the things she saw on the television. She wasn't going to just be able to sit on a throne and look pretty with poise all day. Being Kesh's queen meant leading an entire clan of people she knew almost nothing about. It also meant putting her life on the line for something that she didn't understand. Still, whether she liked it or not, she would go to the end of the world and back for Kesh. The love she felt was like a fire that burned in her chest and, for him, she had already given up her soul.

"Come on, honey," she said while she put Adis in his baby tub. "Let's get all this food from underneath your fat chin. Ooooh, where did all these rolls come from, huh? When did you get so chunky!"

She let him splash the water around for a little bit before she cleaned him all up with her favorite lavender-scented baby soap. By the time she scooped him out of the tub, he wasn't even able to hold his head up any longer. His head flopped on her shoulder and by the time she got him in his pajamas his tiny snores were filling the air. She laid him down in his crib and turned on the baby monitors, placing one on the nightstand and the other in her back pocket, before leaving the room.

Her hunger began to well up inside of her, and she couldn't wait to get to the bag of blood waiting for her on the dinner table. She was sure that Kesh was done with his by now, but when she got back, she smiled. Kesh was sitting at the dinner table with a full bag in front of him. He'd waited for her, although she knew he was hungry too.

"Kesh, you could have eaten," she said taking her seat. "You know I don't like for my king to be hungry."

"And I don't like for my queen to eat by herself," Kesh countered and nodded toward the pouch.

Adirah popped her pouch open and chuckled slightly. "You know when I was younger, my mother wouldn't let us touch our food if we didn't say our grace. I guess it doesn't really matter now."

Her smile was a sad one, as it always was when she thought of her mother. She hadn't seen or spoken to her in over a year, and she really hoped that she was doing all right. Instead of letting her sad thoughts consume her, she dug into her pouch of blood. The craziest thing was that it always tasted as good as steak used to taste to her. It fulfilled her every need and it was almost as if she could never get full off of it.

It took them a matter of five minutes to suck their pouches dry, and when they were done, they wore satisfied expressions on their faces.

Their eyes connected and Adirah's tongue licked the few drops of blood trying to sneak their way out of her mouth. She stood and walked slowly to where Kesh was sitting across from her. With little effort, she pushed his chair out and away from the table so that she could straddle him. His hands found the small of her back as she leaned in to kiss him. The moment their lips were about to connect, Kesh turned his head.

"What is it?" Adirah breathed. "What's wrong? Did I do something to make you unhappy?"

"No, my dear Dira," Kesh said, turning back to her and looking up into her eyes. "You make me the happiest I have ever been in this long life. Before you, I was lonely, empty."

"Then what is it?"

"We need to go back."

"Back where, Kesh?"

"Back to the Sefu."

Adirah leaned back to get a good look at Kesh's face. He hadn't mentioned that name in a while, and the last time he did he had a different tone of voice. "But, are we ready?"

"I fear we may never be ready. They are my clan and, although they are displeased with me, I am still their king."

"What brought this about, Kesh? Just a while ago you said we have to wait until the time is right; now you're saying there is no right time."

"Something is coming."

"Something is coming? What?"

"I feel it. It's a darkness, but I can't make it out or tell what it is. But I can feel it, and I know that I need to be with my clan. Now is the time to make things right."

Before Adirah could respond, she heard a sound coming from her pocket. "The baby must have woken up," Adirah said, taking the white monitor from her pocket. "Let me g—"

"Shhh. Go to sleep. Go to sleep. Go to sleep, little baby."

It felt like Adirah's heart had frozen over listening to the sing-song voice coming from the monitor. She jumped up from Kesh's lap, and both of them moved with a speed faster than the human eye could see, reaching baby Adis's room in seconds. They burst in the door, and Adirah gasped seeing the hooded figure cradling her baby boy. Whoever it was had their back to the door.

Kesh charged toward the figure, but one simple finger flick sent Kesh crashing into the far wall. Instead of sliding down the wall to the ground, Kesh was held there, as if he was pinned.

"Who are you?" Adirah said. "Release my son and I will not kill you."

The figure chuckled, set Adis gently back down in his crib, and slowly removed the hood from their head.

"You wouldn't be able to do that if you tried." The person turned around, revealing a beautiful woman with long dreads pulled back. Her skin glowed, and her fangs glistened in the darkness, revealing her true nature. "I wouldn't even dare you to do that."

"What is it you want?"

"I think the question is, what is it you want?"

"I want to know who the hell you are and why you are here."

"Fair enough," she said in an even voice. "My name is Dena, and I am here to show you who you really are, Adirah Messa."

"What? What do you mean, who I really am?"

"I take it that your lover boy here has not told you the truth about your bloodline. Or why he is so drawn to you." The look on Adirah's face answered the question since her mouth did not. "I didn't think so."

Dena turned to Kesh, who held a shocked expression on his face. He fought against his invisible restraints as the intruder took a few steps toward him, but he could not get free. That was a power that he had never seen before, and he could not understand how she was doing it.

"Kesh, king of the Sefu clan, what a pleasure to finally make your acquaintance. I wish it had been under better circumstances."

"I wish it hadn't been at all!" Kesh snarled.

While Dena's back was turned, Adirah tried to attack her from behind. Bad choice. She was sent flying the same way Kesh had been, and now both of them were pinned on the wall.

"I told you not to try that," Dena said over her shoulder and then turned her attention back to Kesh. "I understand that this may not be as tasteful an entrance as I would have liked. In all honesty, I would have liked to remain a—what do these kids call them these days? Ah, yes—an urban legend. But times call for measures more undesirable. Kesh, I am here to tell you that everything you know about your creation is a lie."

"What do you mean?"

"I mean Adie, your creator, was no princess or queen of the Sefu clan."

"How do you know about Adie? How would you know she was not the daughter of the king of Sefu?"

"I know because Adie was my younger and more reckless sister. So, if she were a princess, I would have been too, right?"

"Sister?"

"You heard me right. Can't you tell by my eyes? Aren't they the same as Adie's? The same as your dear Adirah's?"

Kesh's breathing slowed as he studied her eyes. They were the same shape and color as both Adie's and Adirah's. He gasped and shook his head. "But why would Adie lie about something like that? I don't understand."

"I do not want to wake my greatest nephew, so I will release you both only if you promise to not attack me again."

There was a small pause before Kesh finally nodded, and Adirah did the same behind her. With them still glued to the wall, Dena made her way out of the room. The couple did not fall to the ground until Dena had already turned the corner and was headed toward the living room.

"Greatest nephew?" Adirah tried to ask Kesh, but he rushed out of the room behind Dena.

In the light of the living room, Kesh was able to see that Dena was dressed in casual clothes as well, but over them she wore an old hooded burgundy cloak. She was seated comfortably on the tan love seat and made a motion with her hands toward the couch directly across from her. "Sit."

Adirah didn't know how she felt about being given permission to sit down in her own house, but she also knew that this Dena person was no one to play with. She had powers that not even Kesh possessed.

"If Adie was not the daughter of the king of Sefu, who was she?" Kesh asked as soon as he sat down. He couldn't stand the suspense. He'd just found out that his entire existence was a lie, and a part of his cold heart seemed to be in pieces. "And why couldn't I sense you?"

"Ever since we were little, my sister was always the more outgoing one." Dena gave a small smile. "And when we were turned together it remained that way. We were so special, our existence was supposed to always be kept a secret, but of course, Adie couldn't accept that. She couldn't stand the thought of being kept away from the world we knew so well for eternity, so she left. She went above ground and recruited other lost vampires. They saw that she was more powerful than any other vampire they'd ever seen and they followed her with no question. She fabricated the story about her existence, and they believed her. She helped people with the same brown skin as us fight for their rights to be human." Dena began to laugh and shook her head. "Can you believe that? She fought for the right to be something that she never would be again. And then she met you." Dena's eyes bore into Kesh's, and there were many unspoken words exchanged.

Adirah took notice of this and cleared her throat. "Excuse me. I just have a question: why did you call my son your nephew?"

"Because you, Adirah, are a direct descendent of my sister. Her blood courses strong through your veins."

Adirah's head shook, and she tried to make sense of what that meant. "But I thought vampires couldn't reproduce."

"Not just any vampire; only the one who was given the gift of reproduction from the king of vampires himself. Dracula."

Kesh sat up straight in his seat at the mention of the king of all kings. His brow furrowed in Dena's direction. "That is just a myth."

"You asked why you were not able to sense me, correct?"

"Yes."

"Recite the myth to me."

"'Through the blood of the king of all kings, nine were given life. With the gifts of illusion, telekinesis, fire, ice, clairvoyance, energy snatching, precognition, shapeshifting, and life they are the most powerful of all soldiers. Ancients. The only things that can remove them from earth are if they place their essence inside of another being or from the bite of an Ancient Lykan.'" Kesh stopped reciting in the middle of the myth and put his hands in the air. "What does old folklore have to do with anything?"

"It has everything to do with everything."

"But how?"

Instead of answering, Dena lifted her hand, causing everything in the living room except the couches they were sitting on to rise from the ground. After a few seconds, she drew back her power and allowed everything else to drop back to the ground.

"Telekinesis." Kesh felt all the wind leave him. "You're an Ancient. So, Adie wasn't born a vampire?"

"No. She, just like me, was bitten by Dracula himself."

"She was an Ancient as well?"

"Yes. And so is Adirah; well, a descendent of one. The other vampires think that the key to reproduction lies in you, but it does not. It is in her."

Dena pointed at Adirah who, in turn, pointed at herself in shock. "In me?"

"Yes. It has taken centuries for the gift to present itself again. For years I have acted as a protector of all of my sister's children and their children, but you are the only one with the gift.

It was not by chance that Kesh found you, and in time he himself will tell you what I mean. But you, Adirah Messa, are the only vampire in the world who can give birth to vampire babies. To day walkers. You are the true queen of vampires, Adirah. This all was your fate. And now it's time to fulfill your destiny."

"So there have to be other born vampires if Adie's bloodline has come this far."

"No. Adis is the only born vampire known to our kind. The way it works is tricky. Only the true queen can give birth to a vampire; the other kids had no abilities. All of them were human. None had the thirst for blood. It is something that I have been trying to understand for centuries. But now I understand. But this is not all I have come to tell you. I am afraid I have bad news."

"I think all of this is a little hard to swallow. I don't think anything else you can say would surprise me at this point."

Dena looked back to Kesh, the man whom both her sister and her greatest niece loved. She understood why. He was strong, and his sense of loyalty to his clan radiated from him although they had betrayed him. He was a born leader, and he would do whatever to take care of his family. *Good.*

"You feel it, don't you?" Dena asked him. "That bad feeling in your gut that just won't go away. When you go to sleep and wake up, it's still there. Like something is coming for you."

"Yes," he breathed. "What is it?"

"It's them. They have awakened."

"Who is 'them'?"

"Our mortal enemies: the Ancient Lykans."

"That's a myth. A tale to scare vampires."

"A few moments ago, I was a myth too, right?" When Dena got no response, she continued. "Kesh, it's up to you to unite all vampires against them. Even your personal enemies, the Malum. We cannot fight this war alone. We need every vampire we can get."

"Why me?"

"Adie chose you to be the king of all vampires. You are the Ancients' general and chief. And because, by bringing Adis into the world, you have awakened them. They want him. As long as you stay here, you all are in grave danger."

"Why do they want my son?"

"Because Adis is different from us all. He has a soul."

Chapter 3

Dena told the couple all they needed to know at that moment. She would wait to tell them about the prophecy. She felt that they'd been overwhelmed enough for one night. She could only imagine how Adirah felt seeing a hooded figure holding her child. Dena just hadn't been able to help herself. Although she had plans to present herself by knocking on the front door, she just wanted to see what Adis looked like up close.

She'd seen him many times from afar, and he was cute as a button. Still, that had nothing on what it felt like to hold his little body in her arms. He'd stirred in his sleep and even woken up, but one look into Dena's eyes and he recognized her. Not her, per se, but her eyes. They were his mother's eyes. She allowed Dena to continue holding him and even to put him back to sleep without causing any alarm. He was everything and more. She knew she would do anything and everything to make sure he survived the war.

After her talk with Kesh and Adirah, it was agreed that they would pack as many things as could fit into their backpacks and leave their new life behind. Dena waited patiently until they were done and Adirah appeared back in the living room with the baby in her arms. There had never been a doubt in Dena's mind that Kesh and Adirah would come with her. In all honesty, they didn't have a choice.

"Come," she said waving her arm. "My car is outside."

"You drove?" Adirah asked, causing Dena to chuckle.

"Yes, I did. We are not savages. We have actually adjusted quite well to the change in times."

The night was still when they stepped through the doors and, sure enough, there was a black Mercedes-Benz G wagon parked on the street in front of their home. Kesh took Adirah's bag once Dena unlocked the SUV, and he put both of their bags in the back of it.

"Here." Dena reached for Adis and Adirah held him tighter, leaning back.

"I got it," she responded and stepped around Dena to the open back door.

There was a red car seat back there that Adirah strapped Adis securely into, and she made sure that the seat belt was locked. Her guard was still up when it came to Dena. It wasn't that she didn't trust her, because when she looked at Dena, she saw a piece of herself. Still, Adirah felt as if there was something that was not being said to her. She couldn't put her finger on it, but it just felt like there was an elephant in the room.

"I did not mean to frighten you," Dena told her once Adirah was done. "I just . . . wanted to see him."

Adirah nodded but said nothing. Instead, she opted to climb into the car and step over Adis's dangling legs. Behind her, she heard a small sigh before the door shut. Kesh got in the passenger's seat, and Dena got in the driver's side.

Dena started the car, but just as she was about to pull off, she put her nose in the air, sniffing. It was faint, but the odor was something that she had never been able to miss. When she turned to Kesh, he was doing the same as her. Their eyes connected. They both knew that it could only mean one thing.

"Lykan," they said in unison.

As soon as the word was out in the air, they heard sounds coming from the house, and the living room light flickered on.

"It must have come through the back door," Kesh said. "Our scents are still fresh. It will be able to track us now. I have to kill it."

"No. You take Adirah, and I will handle the creature."

"You are the only one who knows the location of the Ancients," Kesh said, shaking his head. "It is you who must take Dira and the baby."

"Kesh," Adirah breathed sharply. She too smelled the foul odor. It was one she'd never experienced. She'd heard from the stories Kesh told her how fierce those of Lykan blood were, and just knowing that one was in her home looking for them was unsettling to her. "No. Let's just go."

"It will follow us, Dira." Kesh turned in his seat and placed a hand gently on her face. "This is the only way to ensure our safety for now. I will find you."

He turned back to Dena and nodded, giving her the silent okay to go. He got out of the car and walked toward the house. He was dressed like the typical mortal man in a gray Nike jogger sweat suit, with white tennis shoes on his feet. He was able to move easily, and when he heard the car pull off, he made to open the front door. He could tell that the Lykan sensed him as well and there was no purpose in trying a sneak attack. He twisted the doorknob and stepped into the front hallway of the home.

"Well, well, well," a raspy voice greeted him. "If it isn't Kesh of the Sefu clan."

Standing exactly twenty feet away from him was a muscular man. He had coffee-colored skin and a black connected beard that matched the short hair on his head. His eyes, like all Lykan eyes, were the color of a phoenix's fire. Although he was not in his Lykan form, his canines were naturally sharp.

"Long time no see, Willeth," Kesh said calling him by his human name.

"Not since the last time we battled."

"And I won," Kesh reminded him.

"You got lucky that time," Willeth said flexing his muscles in his black T-shirt. He studied Kesh, looking him up and down, and gave a laugh that was mixed with a snarl. "I never thought that I'd ever see you look so weak. So human."

"Times have changed." Kesh shrugged. "I have found that it is easier to endure this eternal life if I can fit in. Too many eyes on you can be a bad thing. Also, looks can be very deceiving. Now, Willeth, tell me why you are here."

"I am here because you have something that we want."

"My son."

"Ding! Ding! Where is he?"

"You can't have him," Kesh growled.

"When I take him back to my master, it will be your fault," Willeth taunted Kesh. "Don't you know that? You have given birth to the first vampire ever to have a soul. Haven't you ever read the prophecy?"

Kesh couldn't hide the surprised look on his face.

"Well, of course you haven't. Because if you did, I'm sure you and your precious lady friend would have thought twice before you brought the little slugger into the world. I'll make this easy for you. If you hand him over, I will be sure to make the deaths of you and your lady friend . . . Adirah, right? I will make your deaths as quick and painless as possible."

"You will not hurt my family. I defeated you before. I can do it again."

"That," Willeth said, chuckling, before throwing his arms to his sides and crouching slightly, "was before I drank the blood of an Ancient!"

He threw his head back and howled and began to transform right before Kesh's eyes. Kesh could tell that he was different, bigger, fiercer. That wasn't something that could just happen to a beast like him. Only a powerful magic could change a Lykan's transformed body.

Kesh did the same thing. He quickly removed his jacket and the T-shirt that he was wearing.

His transformation was quicker, and he felt his muscles grow bigger and his nails longer. His deadly fangs poked out from his mouth, and he felt every one of his senses heighten. He was at full power since he'd just fed, but still, he knew that battle was going to take something out of him.

In werewolf form, Willeth could not speak, but he didn't have to. The thirst for blood in his eyes told Kesh all that he needed to know. Willeth was a sight to see. The claws on his feet bore down on the ground, and the long claws on his fingers were sharp enough to impale two bodies at the same time. He charged toward Kesh and swiped one of his hands at him ferociously, but Kesh jumped up onto the ceiling.

Willeth jumped and tried to grab Kesh; however, he fell to the ground behind the beast and punched him in the spine. The blow was a powerful one and should have sent Willeth flying in the total opposite direction; instead, he only stumbled a bit. Kesh followed through with his hand and swiped the beast's face when it tried to take a chunk out of Kesh's arm. It howled loudly and tried to blink away the blood seeping into its eyes. Kesh tried to go in for another attack, but Willeth was ready for him that time. He grabbed Kesh's attacking hand and flung the vampire so hard that he went through the walls of the living room and the bathroom. He crashed into the sink, cracking it and causing water to begin to spout.

With no time to catch his breath, he was up again on the defense as Willeth came plummeting through the walls as well. His howl sounded as he brought his claws down across Kesh's chest and stomach, spraying blood on the tiled walls of the bathroom.

"Ahhh!"

Kesh had never felt a burning pain like that before. He didn't understand, but it was like Willeth's claws made him weak. As if they'd been dipped in the one thing that could poison him: holy water. He tried to fend off each attack, but Willeth had taken full advantage of Kesh's weakening state.

After flinging him around a few more times, Willeth finally grabbed Kesh by the neck in the hallway. Sliding him up the wall and cutting off his airway, Willeth roared in Kesh's face spraying him with saliva. Kesh watched in horror as Willeth's already-sharp teeth grew sharper, and more teeth grew around them. Just as it was about to go in for the kill, Kesh felt his neck be released, and he dropped to the floor. Willeth flew back almost as if the wind had taken him, and he landed with the whimper of a hurt dog. Kesh didn't see it but, shortly after Willeth's landing, he heard the sickening crack of a neck being broken.

Kesh heard something coming his way, and he tried to stand up to defend himself, but he was too weak. He fell back down, but before he hit the ground, he felt a set of arms catch him.

"Kesh, are you injured badly?"

Kesh looked up and saw that he was staring into Dena's face. She held a look of concern and her brow furrowed at his still-exposed wounds.

"Why are you healing so slowly?" she asked. "This is why I told you to let me handle it. Now not only is your scent here, but so is your blood. You need to feed."

"The garage," he said fraily, pointing in the garage's direction. "There is food there."

Dena laid him down gently and hurried in the direction he'd pointed. When she returned, she carried on her shoulder a cooler that she must have gotten from the garage. It looked to be full of ice and every pouch of blood that was in the freezer.

"Here." Dena placed one to his lips. "We must hurry. When he does not return with any news at all, they will send a whole fleet. We must go."

She didn't have to tell him twice. His animalistic senses kicked in at the smell of mortal blood, and he downed the entire pouch in seconds. It gave him just enough energy to stand up and walk without swaying; however, his wounds still had not healed fully. Dena helped him outside to the SUV. After storing the cooler in the very back, she then went back to the house once he was safely inside.

"Kesh!" Adirah cried when he got inside and she saw the shape he was in.

"I'm all right," Kesh told her and tried to give her a weak smile. "Dena came right in the nick of time."

"We had only gotten to the end of the block when she turned around. She said that you didn't know what you were getting yourself into."

"She was right," Kesh said, thinking back to the strength of Willeth and the way his claws affected him.

"You need to feed!" Adirah said staring at wide gashes on his chest.

"I have," Kesh told her.

"Then why haven't you healed?"

"I am," Kesh said. "It's just happening more slowly this time."

In his peripheral vision, he saw a flash of red, and he smelled smoke. He whipped his head back to the direction of the house and saw that it was going up in flames.

The driver-side door opened and Dena hopped in. "They won't have your scent or be able to taste your blood now."

"Taste his blood?"

"Ancient Lykans, like Ancient vampires, can see a person's entire life just by one drop of blood. There are things in your mind, Kesh, and you may not even know how valuable they are until someone else has them. Now, let's get you all to safety. There are many things left to tell you."

Her eyes once again fell on his battle wounds. She'd had centuries to work on her poker face, but at that moment she could not hide the clench in her jaw. Time was not on her side; the full moon was only two weeks away. That was when the war would happen. The Lykans would be at full power, and that was when she was sure they would strike.

Chapter 4

Back in North Carolina

"What's on your mind?"

Tiev almost didn't hear the feminine voice speaking to him. He was so lost in his own thoughts that he had forgotten where he even was. It wasn't until he moved his legs that he felt the warm silk sheets underneath them. He'd been lying on his back with his eyes closed, but he opened them when he felt the hand on his bare shoulder. The first sight to his eyes was the high ceiling; it wasn't until he turned his head on the soft pillow under his head that he saw the beauty lying next to him. Her skin was so light that during the time of slavery she'd always been able to pass. Her long sandy brown hair hung with the ends damp from the sweat that had been on her shoulders. Her eyes penetrated him as if searching for the soul that he didn't have, and her full pink lips offered a smile.

"You've never been this quiet after we made love. Did I do something to displease you?"

Tiev reached to caress her face gently. "No, Risa, you were perfect. As you always are when we make love."

"Then what is it?"

"You aren't her." His simple honesty came out harshly, but there was no other way to put it.

Risa, who understood what the situation would be when she got involved with Tiev, just nodded. Although his words felt like a blow, she knew from the beginning that she would have to work to win the love of a man still in love with a dead vampire.

"No, I am not Vila. I am Risa. Someone you can feel, touch, and who will love you back."

Blow for blow. Tiev felt it in his gut. It was no secret to the entire Sefu clan that Vila had always been in love with Kesh. She was so focused on the king that she didn't notice Tiev's infatuation with her. For years they worked side by side and built a close friendship, but still, Vila only cared about Kesh, even after he bedded her and threw her to the side like a plaything. The only time she returned his attention was when she felt betrayed by Kesh. In a sense, Tiev felt betrayed by Kesh too. He was able to throw centuries of hard work away behind a mortal woman. He put the entire Sefu clan at risk by allowing her in their midst and, for that, he sided with Vila to overthrow him as king. Also, he couldn't lie: he was very infatuated with the thought of being able to reproduce. A child was something he'd always wanted, ever since he was a mortal.

When Vila was killed, he vowed to avenge her death, but now he had an even bigger objective. He didn't want to just destroy Kesh for her; he wanted to kill Kesh for his title. The Sefu needed a stronger ruler, mentally and physically. All he needed to do was feed from Kesh's blood, as Adirah had, and he would be just as powerful.

"I apologize," Tiev said turning to Risa. "You are right. Absolutely right. Maybe it is time that I let go of the past."

"The past," Risa said with wonder in her eyes. "We have come a long way from the coffin days. Haven't we?"

"Yes," Tiev agreed and pulled the comforter up so that his shoulders were covered. "After feeling these fabrics, I don't know how I ever went without them for so long. Who wants a cramped coffin when I can have a king-sized bed?"

"The only kind of bed for a king. The future king of the Sefu."

"I love the sound of that," Tiev said.

And he truly did. Hearing those words come from her mouth aroused him. His thick, eight-inch member rose to attention, and he grabbed her forcefully, positioning her on top of him. She straddled him, and his strong hands rested on her wide hips. He growled in a low tone.

"You want me to fuck you again, King?" Risa whispered sexily down into his face.

The tip of his penis was at her wet opening, and he yearned to feel it completely inside of her. He nodded and moaned as she eased herself down on him, gasping from the pleasurable feeling.

"You fill me up, King. Do you know that?" she said as she began to bounce up and down on top of him. "I'm going to do you better than Vila ever could have, okay? I want to be your queen. Can I be that, Tiev?"

Tiev was in a blissful trance. At that moment, he would have given her anything she asked for. The feeling of her breasts pressed against his chest, mixed with the feeling he was getting down below, had him ready to explode. He allowed her to sex his thoughts away and, by the time he climaxed, Vila was the furthest thing from his mind.

Chapter 5

Young Lykan Cairo did not want to be the deliverer of bad news, but it was inevitable. As he walked through the dim halls of the Lykan mansion on the outskirts of Tennessee, he practiced the words he was going to say. It had been a while since he, or any of the others, had had a place they could call home: a place where they were able to walk around in their wolf forms freely, and a place where meals were not scarce. Six months prior, he himself had been homeless, wandering the world, not able to control the beast inside of him. The killing and feeding was all he knew for so long. Since he'd been turned the year prior, that was. His life seemed pointless until he got the call, until every Lykan in the surrounding five states got the call for that matter. An Ancient Lykan had been awakened.

Cairo had been one of the soldiers sent to scope out why Willeth had not returned when he was supposed to. When they arrived at what was supposed to be the residence of the king of the Sefu clan, all they were met with were the remains of the home and a Lykan skeleton. The vampires were long gone, and so was their scent. Since Cairo was the youngest, the other Lykans often treated him as disposable. They made him the deliverer of bad news, knowing what could possibly happen to him.

"Just breathe, Cairo. Everything will be okay," he said to himself as he walked down the long hall. He heard a roar of laughter from the dinner hall below, and he knew that the others were having the time of their life. "You know, maybe you'll be able to go down there after you tell the Ancient One the news. Yeah, maybe you'll be able to enjoy a nice tall glass of your favorite vodka."

He reached the tall closed door where he knew the Ancient One was. There was a wolf door knocker that he reached to grab, but his presence was already known.

"Come in, young one."

The voice boomed so loudly in his head that he had to wonder if he'd heard it out loud. Slowly, he turned the handle and pushed the door open. He entered the room, purposely leaving the door open as he took a few steps inside. He had to force himself not to jump when he heard the door slam behind him.

How did that happen?

The temperature in the room was warm, but for some reason, he felt cold. The room was big, bigger than any master bedroom he'd ever seen, complete with a library in the corner, a tall chair resembling a throne, and a fireplace in front of it. The chair was facing the opposite way and whoever was sitting in it was breathing heavily, like a beast, and watching the flame.

"You have news about the prophecy child?"

The voice was so loud, it was like something he'd heard in a nightmare. He heard a scratching sound, like a nail scratching a board repeatedly. He cleared his throat and bowed once. "Y . . . yes, Ancient One."

Cairo heard him begin to sniff the air, as if something about the newcomer was off. "You are not the soldier I sent to handle the job. The one I allowed to taste my blood."

"No, I am not him, Ancient One. That was Willeth."

"And you are?"

"Cairo. My name is Cairo."

"Your blood is fresh. You aren't even a year old. How were you able to hear my call?"

Cairo was shocked. He didn't understand what the Ancient One meant by that. He was under the impression that any Lykan in the surrounding states had heard the call. "I was under the impression that all Lykans could hear the call if they are near. And if they are far then they can feel you."

"Only the most powerful of my kind can hear my call. You smell weak."

"I . . ."

"Where is the soldier I sent? The one you call Willeth."

"Dead, sir. I mean, Ancient One. It seems as if he may have been ambushed."

"Ambushed?"

The way his voice carried made the young Lykan subconsciously take a step back, but it was too late. The Ancient One moved with speed unseen, and before Cairo knew it, he was being pinned on a wall by the biggest beast he'd ever seen in his life. He himself was a werewolf, but he'd never seen another look as frightening as the one before him. It was seven feet tall, thick black and gold fur coated its body, and the sharp teeth were as long as half of his human arm. Its eyes were the color of fire, and now Cairo understood why it felt as if he were hearing the voice in his mind: because he was.

"What do you mean, ambushed!" The voice sounded again, but the mouth never moved. Saliva and snot from the beast sprayed on Cairo's face.

Cairo tried to speak, but his airway was completely closed. The beast's paws were the same size as his whole torso. Its fingers were wrapped so tightly around Cairo's neck that the long claws were digging into his shoulders. Just when he was sure to pass out, Cairo was released and dropped to the ground with a loud thud.

Cairo grabbed his throbbing neck and gasped for air. Out of the corner of his eye, he saw the beast get smaller until he was just a man. He watched the bare feet walk toward the large bed, and the man threw on long red silk robes.

"Leave me."

That time the voice was aloud. It wasn't too deep, but it wasn't high pitched, either. It was just smooth. Cairo struggled to his feet, too fearful to even look behind him at the face of the man.

"Let me get that for you," the Ancient One said.

The door flung open, and Cairo hurried to it. He couldn't get out of there fast enough.

Chapter 6

There will be one born to vampire who will be able to walk in the daylight and drink the blood of mortals at his own will. He is one who all vampirekind must protect with their most precious of life, for his is more important. For his blood has the power to turn the darkest inhuman of hearts mortal again.

Chapter 7

It took an entire day to reach their destination, and they arrived at night. Kesh was the one who'd taught Adirah that not everything was what it seemed, but when they reached the snowy mountains in Colorado, he was confused. On the ride, his wounds still had not healed completely, but he'd put on another shirt to cover them. "Where are we?"

Dena smiled at him and got out of the car. "Home," she said, and he followed her.

In the back seat, Adirah glanced out the window and looked up at the snowy mountains. She understood why Dena had the thick cloak on, and she realized that they hadn't packed any winter clothes since it was still so hot outside. She turned her attention to her sleeping son and leaned down to kiss his forehead. He had been such a big boy on the ride and had only fussed a few times.

She sighed. "I'm sorry, baby boy," she whispered. "This isn't the life I wanted for you. But we will do everything to protect you." She looked out the window again. "Even climb a tall, snowy mountain, apparently."

She got out of the car and wasn't prepared for the nip at her ears or the snow on her exposed toes in her sandals. She gave a small shriek, and Dena laughed at her.

"Even vampires get cold."

"Cold is an understatement."

"You remind me of Adie and me when we were first brought here. But no worries; you won't need thick clothes where we're going."

"This experience isn't anything like the stories I read when I was younger," Adirah complained.

"Most things are correct. They left out the most important thing, though."

"And what's that?"

Dena didn't answer her. Instead, she trudged through the snow toward the base of the mountain they'd stopped next to. She placed her palm on it and closed her eyes. The place where her hand was glowed a vibrant orange before the entire mountain rippled like water. She looked back at Adirah and smiled.

"The magic." She motioned for them all to get back into the SUV, and once they were inside, she drove through the mountain. "It is only a fifteen-second window."

Adirah looked back at the mountain and watched the entire thing fade until she was looking into nothing but clear skies. She had a feeling that she wasn't even in Denver anymore.

"We just drove through a mountain," Adirah said. "I don't think anything is going to surprise me after this."

"Except maybe a castle on a hill?"

"A castle on the wh . . ." Adirah didn't need to finish her sentence. The shock on her face turned into a broad smile. "Magic."

The craziest thing about everything that was happening was that in her mortal life she never knew of any of the things, the beautiful things, that were hidden in the shadows. Ever since she'd been turned, it was like she learned something new every day. It was amazing to think that just two years ago she didn't believe in the things that went bump in the night. Now she couldn't imagine life without Kesh or baby Adis.

Dena drove the SUV all the way to a tall metal gate that lifted the moment they got there. "We are here," Dena said, cutting the car off and stepping out.

As soon as her feet touched the ground at least five other vampires, men and women, came to her aid. They bowed to her, and she smiled at them all as they welcomed her home. When

Kesh and Adirah got out of the car, the group of vampires did not acknowledge them. However, when Adirah scooped Adis into her arms and brought him into their view, everything got quiet. Their eyes on her son made Adirah wary to take another step.

"Do not worry," Dena said. "There are no savages here. They have never seen a baby vampire before. Or anything like him for that matter. Come."

Kesh took Adirah by the hand and guided her through the forming crowd of vampires and across the grassy plain to the castle. It was strange: he'd been through many centuries of life, and it was like the castle had a little piece of each century. Still, it was obvious that it had been modernized. Once they stepped through the tall double doors, his favorite scent in the whole world hit his nostrils.

"Butterscotch?"

"Funny," Dena said, closing the doors behind her, "I smell clean linen this time. What do you smell, Adirah?"

Adirah inhaled and laughed slightly, bewildered. "I smell baby Adis's bath soap. But, how?"

"This castle is one of the many wonders of the world. It was created by a very old magic no longer practiced by witches. Our maker asked for it to be made for us and it has provided us shelter from the outside world for almost our entire existence. One of its wonders is that you will smell a different scent every time you enter, always one of your favorites. This way."

She led them through the large castle and on the way they passed a number of vampires, all dressed in modern clothes. The entire place was like something out of a movie and Adirah couldn't help but be in awe of it all, from the elegant fixtures to the famous paintings that decorated the walls. The floors were wooden, and the windows were crystal. She lost count of how many fountains she passed and how many room doors. It seemed as if the castle would never end. She didn't even know how Dena knew where she was going.

"Years of practice." Dena winked at her.

Adirah gasped, realizing that she could read her mind. "But, Kesh can't read my mind. How can you?"

"I am an Ancient, my dear. I can do a lot of things that Kesh cannot do, or you for that matter. But you will learn."

As they walked, Adirah asked with the excitement of a child in her voice, "Is it true that you all once battled the Ancient Lykans? I remember hearing those stories when I was first turned.

Back then it all just sounded like myths, but now I'm thinking they weren't."

"It is true." Dena nodded, but her eyes seemed to glaze over, as if she was thinking of something that she would much rather forget. "There were five of them. More powerful than any Lykan you've ever seen."

"Like Willeth?"

"Twenty times more powerful than Willeth."

"How did they get here? The same as the Ancients?"

"No one knows exactly how they got here, but the Ancient Lykans were a threat to everyone. Not just vampires. There was a time when they were at war with the witches, and after too many of them were murdered they decided to create a monster thirsty for blood."

"Dracula."

"Yes. They made my creator, and he was the first of our kind. He had the witches' magic in his veins, which made him the most powerful vampire. Yet, as powerful as he was, he was still not strong enough to defeat all five of them by himself. So, he created us. Together, we were able to destroy three of them, but the last two were the most powerful."

"What happened to them?"

"We weakened them enough to the point where the witches were able to put them into a deep slumber."

"At the house, Willeth said he drank from the blood of an Ancient. If they are all asleep, how is this possible?"

Dena looked from Kesh to Adirah, and the look on her face was not readable. Kesh felt the hairs on the back of his neck sit up, and he knew instantly that whatever she had to say would not be good.

"When you meet the other Ancient vampires, it will all be explained."

"Where are you taking us?" Kesh asked, not accepting her answer. "What will be explained?"

They reached a door at the end of a hall on the second floor. It was slightly ajar as if whoever was inside it was waiting for them. The light inside was dimmed, and there were murmurs coming from it. Before entering, Dena glanced back at baby Adis, and a hint of wonder crossed her eyes.

"The prophecy," she said, before walking across the threshold of the doors.

Chapter 8

"So it is true," said the Ancient introduced to Kesh as Tep, as he stared at Adis.

The baby had to have sensed the power in the room because as soon as they'd entered the room, he woke up. He now sat in his mother's arms staring at the new faces around the round table. There was a candle in front of Adirah's spot, and she naturally pushed it out of Adis's reach. The last thing she needed was for any of his beautiful curls to be set on fire.

Dena introduced everyone, but it was obvious that the other Ancients couldn't care less about Kesh or Adirah. Their infatuation was with the baby vampire in the room. Adirah didn't like the way their eyes lingered on him. It was almost as if they were dissecting him with their eyes.

"Yes, Tep," Constance said in wonder. "Just like the prophecy says."

"A baby vampire," Eron muttered.

"Who can walk in the sun without a magic ring."

"He's so cute!"

"Lira!"

"What? He is cute!"

Tep shook his head at Lira and then turned his attention to Dena. "What all have you told them?"

"Just what they needed to know until now."

"Nothing of the prophecy?"

"No. I figured I'd leave that up to you."

Kesh didn't like that he was being talked about as if he were not in the room. "What prophecy?"

"The one about your son," Lira told him. "Have you ever heard of something called a 'golden child'?"

"Yes."

"Well, he's more like the 'black child.' And I'm not talking about his skin."

"Lira!" Tep groaned again.

"What! It's true! He's a cute little chocolate baby," Lira said. Her short haircut fit her heart-shaped face perfectly. The bangs in the front came down to her chin, and when she focused her attention back to Kesh, she brushed them away from her eyes. "Your son is very special."

"Because he has a soul."

"That is one reason, yes. The other is, well, Tep?" Lira looked to Tep in hopes that he would jump in, and he did just that.

"The prophecy was written long ago by the witches. It was the only way to ensure that the spell they used on the Ancient Lykans would make them stay asleep forever. They thought for sure it was foolproof."

"Thought?" Adirah finally found her voice.

"Yes. They had no clue that one of the gifts Dracula gave us would be the gift of life. They counted on the fact that no vampire could reproduce, and now, well, we have your son here."

"What does the prophecy say?" Adirah asked.

"'There will be one born to vampire who will be able to walk in the daylight and drink the blood of mortals at his own will. He is one who all vampirekind must protect with their most precious of life, for his is more important. For his blood has the power to turn the darkest inhuman of hearts mortal again.'"

When Tep got done reciting the prophecy the entire room grew silent. Adirah's breath slowed, and her wide eyes found her love's. She wanted Kesh to say something to ease her mind but, from the looks of it, he was holding the same bewildered expression. Tep's voice seemed to linger in the air, and his words played over again in her head: *"For his blood has the power to turn the darkest inhuman of hearts mortal again."*

She listened to her son coo and "aw" at the people in the room, not knowing what exactly was going on or being said. He was bubbly and happy.

"What does his birth have to do with the Ancient Lykans waking up?" Kesh wanted to know.

"By him being born, the curse was broken. One of them is already awake," Dena said, and that struck up alarm across the table.

"How do you know this?" the Ancient known as Brax asked.

"Upon retrieving them to bring them here, we were attacked."

"By an Ancient Lykan?"

"No, but a Lykan nonetheless. He was stronger than the rest, but not as strong as an Ancient. He told Kesh that he'd drunk the blood of one, though."

"That can only mean that one of them has awakened," Rain said, pushing her long, thick braids to the back of her head and rubbing her dark hands together.

"But which one?" Eron asked. "Mezza or Tidas?"

"I don't know," Dena answered. "I killed the beast before he could take Kesh's head off his shoulders."

It was obvious that Kesh was embarrassed. After Adie turned him, he was used to being the most respected and powerful vampire in the room. Right then he felt like a peon next to giants. Granted, he was thankful to Dena for saving his life; he just couldn't get it out of his head that he wasn't able to defeat a Lykan, of all things. He'd defeated and killed many of them in his time as king of the Sefu. However, his most powerful punch barely made Willeth budge. If that was what just drinking from an Ancient Lykan could do, he didn't want to think about what fighting a real one would be like.

"There is something else," Dena said. Using her speed, she went from her chair across from Kesh to standing right beside him in the blink of an eye. She grabbed the bottom of the T-shirt he'd put on, and she lifted it, exposing his wounds to the room. "After being attacked by the Lykan, his regeneration powers are going very slowly."

"I have heard of this, but surely . . . No, it can't be." Xion shook his head. His long hair was combed neatly up into a bun on his head. His handsome face held nothing but worry, like he was trying to make sense of something that he didn't understand. "It just cannot be."

"What cannot be, brother? Speak," Tep goaded him.

"I have heard stories, from the vampires we allow to come and go, that there are some Lykans who dip their claws in holy water before battling vampires. It weakens them by interfering with their ability to heal during the battle and makes it easier for the beast to go in for the kill."

"Shit," Tep said under his breath. "And if they know about the baby already, then they are already preparing for war. They will stop at nothing to get him."

"Why?" Adirah asked. "He's just a baby. He has nothing to do with this war."

"That is where you are wrong, my dear Adirah," Dena said releasing Kesh's shirt. "He has everything to do with this war, for a single drop of his blood would turn an Ancient Lykan or vampire mortal. We would die instantly. The Lykans have always been thirsty for power, and they will dispose of anything that will get in their way. Especially a little vampire baby who can do what it took us a whole war to do."

"So what do we do?" Kesh asked after another moment of silence passed.

"We will train you both in the way of the Ancients. You must learn to fight like us if you wish to survive. But even with the two of you, that will not be enough."

"I will recruit my clan, the Sefu!"

"Yes." Dena nodded. "But we will also need the Malum."

"What?" Adirah sneered. "They tried to kill us."

"Only because of a long, drawn-out, petty feud between the two kings," Tep spat. "When I was created, all vampires were brothers and sisters. None opposed each other." He paused to give Kesh a knowing glance. "And none broke the law to kill each other."

"Vila would have murdered us, including my unborn child. What she did was an act of treason, punishable by death." Kesh's voice was icy. He didn't care that Tep could probably snap him in two. He didn't like his tone. He was starting to get the feeling that maybe his family wasn't wanted, and suddenly he felt on edge. "If the prophecy says my son can turn anyone mortal, including Ancients, what do you want him here for? How do I know that you aren't trying to kill us?"

"Because Dena will rip out all of our throats if we harm a hair on any of your heads," Lira said with a shrug. "Plus, I like the little baby. I may fight anyone who tries to hurt him too." She smiled at baby Adis, and he returned it with a wide grin of his own.

"Tep is the only one who has an issue," Constance spoke up. "He always acts like he has a stone stuck up his ass."

"I don't have anything stuck up my ass!" Tep snapped. "I just know we only have two weeks until the full moon. That is when the Lykans will be at full power. Do we really think that he will present an army of enough vampires ready to fight for the cause by that time?"

"You're asking us," Dena said. She'd reclaimed her seat and was leaning forward with her hands clasped together. "Shouldn't you be asking him?"

All eyes went to Kesh and his went to Adirah, who too was looking at him. With all her heart she wanted to think that what they said wasn't true, but deep down she knew it was. She heard it in all of their voices. She'd always known her son was special, and always wondered why he wasn't born with the thirst. Kesh's prediction about that had been slightly right, just missing a few details. Never in her right mind would she have thought that her baby would have a soul. When she gave birth to him, she was sure she was giving birth to a child doomed for eternity. She wondered how he would grow. Would he be a child forever? Would he reach a certain age and then stop outwardly growing? She never shared these thoughts with Kesh, for fear of worrying an already-worried mind.

"Kesh," she said and reached for his hand. She sensed his hesitation and knew it could only be at the thought of calling a truce with the Malum.

In all honesty, it made her sick to her stomach. Calum most likely wanted her head on a stick, and Adirah wished that she just would have finished the job when she had the chance. She had no idea how they would turn enemies into allies, but something would have to give. "We have to try. For Adis's sake."

"I know," Kesh said. He sighed deeply, wishing everyone would stop looking at him like he was some unearthly creature.

"You are an unearthly creature," Lira said with a grin.

Kesh couldn't help returning it.

"So what is it, Kesh? Is this something that you will be able to accomplish or not?" Tep's voice was loud and impatient.

Kesh opened his mouth to tell him to give them their bags so they could leave. But suddenly a thought came to his mind. *The elixir!* It was tucked safely in a pocket in the front of the bag he'd packed. While he knew that he did not have enough for the entire Malum clan, he had enough to force Talum to listen to reason. After that, he could only hope for the best.

"One," he started, "you all have to agree and give me your word that you will never read my mind again. Two, my answer is yes. I will deliver you a full army filled with both the Sefu clan and the Malum clan."

Chapter 9

"Number twenty-eight!" a woman's voice called out in the small, family-owned coffee shop.

When no one answered, Lina stepped away from the counter and went back to the register to check the name on the order. She could have sworn that the young man hadn't left as she made his bagel and coffee. It was almost noon, and she groaned at the thought of having to throw away yet another bagel. She, once again, had forgotten to take the money first before she prepared the order. Her manager, Mr. Meyer, would definitely have her ass if he did an inventory count and the drawers didn't match up with the product he had left.

She hated her job and never in a million years thought that she would end up working in a coffee shop. But after dropping out of Billet, she

lost her full-ride scholarship and was subjected
to attend the local community college. She also
didn't have a choice but to get a job so that
she was able to afford her small one-bedroom
apartment and other expenses. Still, that was
better than attending a school full of vampires.
She couldn't even think about stepping foot on
that campus again after all of the things she had
witnessed. Not only that, but she had slept with
one of them. It sucked knowing that he had only
used her to get to who he really wanted. She
really liked him, and she thought that maybe
he liked her too. After finding out what he really
was, all of that went out the window. He left her
high and dry to get her wrist broken and almost
get murdered.

Ever since the incident, she was paranoid in
all that she did. In the back of her mind, she
always wondered if one of them would come
to finish the job. So far it had been a year, and
nobody had come looking for her. Still, her curi-
osity drove her mad with wanting knowledge
about them. She'd grown to despise them and
wanted to know how to kill them, just in case
she was forced to defend herself. It seemed as
if everything in folklore would work, besides

garlic. However, the stake through the heart, holy water, and exposure to sunlight should work. The only thing she didn't understand was how they could walk around completely exposed in the sun.

She sighed at the empty restaurant, but still, she called the name on the order one more time. "Ramel Preston?" she called. "Although I know you aren't here! Ramel Preston."

"I'm so sorry about that!" The voice shocked her, and she couldn't help but jump. "I'm sorry, I didn't mean to frighten you."

"You didn't frighten me," she said looking at him. "Shocked would be a better word to use." She realized she was looking at the guy who had placed the order and she wondered if she took notice of how good-looking he was the first time. Probably not, since she was looking at the cash register instead of his face.

He had chocolaty brown skin that looked like it tasted oh so lovely. His lips were full, and he had a square forehead. He wore his hair in a perfectly lined-up short high-top cut. He wasn't super muscular, but he wasn't at all skinny. His eyes were the same brown as the silk fitted shirt he was wearing and the matching loafers on his feet. He had a little peach fuzz on his chin, and when he smiled at her, his dimples spoke words that he didn't say.

"Well, I'm sorry for shocking you, Lina."

"How do you know my name?" Lina asked, still transfixed by his good looks.

"Um, it's on your name tag," Ramel said grinning.

"Oh." Lina could have kicked herself; that's how stupid she felt. "Duh."

"It's just one of those days," he said and dug into his pocket to pull out some cash. "Here's a twenty. You can keep the change. I believe in tipping for good service."

His baritone voice carried an easygoing tone, and Lina almost didn't hear what he had just said. When she finally did comprehend it, she shook her head when she took the money. "Your stuff is only five bucks. What did I do to deserve a fifteen dollar tip?"

"Well, I'm new in town, and you are the most beautiful woman I've seen so far. That alone deserves that whole twenty. If you get off soon and aren't busy, I'd like to take you somewhere nice."

Lina felt herself blushing, but she didn't say anything. Instead, she cashed him out and handed the money to him. He stared at her hand like he was confused why she was giving the money back.

"Here, just take it," she said and rolled her eyes. "Guys like you come in here all the time trying their luck with me. One, I'm not going to be bought with fifteen dollars. And this isn't the movies; you can't just ask a girl you've just met out on a date."

"Why not?" Ramel said, still not taking the money.

"Because you just don't. What if I were crazy? Or a murderer? Or a—"

"A vampire?" he finished, eyeing her curiously.

"N . . . now, why would you say a vampire?"

"This is not my first time seeing you, Lina," Ramel said to her, ignoring her question. "I have come here before, while you were on break. I have seen what you look up in all of your free time."

"Umm, that's kind of creepy," Lina couldn't stop herself from saying. Then she lied through her teeth. "Everyone knows that vampires don't exist. Why would I be looking up those kinds of things?"

"You know, just like I know, that that is a lie," Ramel said and leaned on the counter. "I know you have seen them before. I know that whatever you saw must haunt your dreams."

"How do you know about vampires?" Lina asked. "Is that why you came into the shop today when no one else is around?"

"Yes," he answered truthfully. "I know about them, and I have vowed to make every last one of them pay."

"So, are you a vampire hunter or something?"

"Are you ready to know that?"

When Lina hesitated, Ramel balled up her still-extended hand and pushed it back toward her. "When you are ready, please come and find me. I will tell you everything." He reached in his pocket and pulled out a motel card. He handed the card to her. "This is where I'm staying for the next few nights."

Lina just nodded, gave him the things he paid for, and watched him exit without another word to her. Glancing down at the card she saw that it was a hotel not too far from where she was working. She only had an hour left in her shift and, although she knew she could go home, if she went there she would just be alone and miserable. Like always.

"The Chase Motel, huh?"

***

One o'clock couldn't come fast enough for Lina. She was slightly irritated when she had to wait an extra fifteen minutes to leave, since her coworker, Steve, was late for his shift. She heard the bell on the business's door as it opened and when she looked up, she had never been happier to see his disheveled hair or his doofy glasses.

"Sorry, Lina! Traffic was a bitch on the way here!"

"On your bike?" Lina raised her eyebrow at him.

"The people wouldn't get out of my way." He shrugged his shoulders and gave a sheepish grin. "Thanks for holding things down until I got here. I know you may have things to handle; pretty girls always do."

Through her irritation, Lina was able to offer him a smile. It was always obvious since her first day of working there that Steve had the biggest crush on her. Although she would never be able to return his affection, she was flattered nonetheless. In reality, that was the first time since she'd met him that he had even been late for work.

"No problem, Steve," Lina said gathering her things. "You have a good day, you hear?"

"You too, my beautiful buttercup."

Lina had made it to the front door of the building and paused with her back to him. Her face was twisted up, and she almost turned back and said something to him. "Yeah, just gonna ignore that," she said and left.

Her car was parked in one of the two employee spots: a small gold Honda Civic. Even though the motel was in walking distance, she didn't want to leave her car at the coffee shop. Who knew? Steve might try to break in it in hopes of finding some panties to sniff.

It didn't take long for her to reach the motel. Minus the few cars that were parked there, it was pretty much vacant. It wasn't a bad-looking motel, which was always surprising to Lina. She always thought of motels as infested with rats and roaches. This one looked like the management actually kept up the property.

She pulled the motel card from the pocket of her jeans and looked at the back of it in hopes that the room number would be on it. Indeed, it was. "Room 215," she said out loud to herself until she found it. She parked not too far away from the room and got out of the car.

Before she even reached the door, it opened. "Well, that didn't take long at all," Ramel said with a smile.

"Were you watching me through the window?"

"Not until I heard your loud-ass muffler pull up while I was trying to nap."

"Oh," Lina said and pointed behind her with one of her thumbs. "I can go. I didn't mean to wake you up."

"No, no." He shook his head and stepped out of the way so that she could enter. "Come on in."

Hesitantly, she did as he said. She didn't know him from a can of paint to trust him, but she was already there. No turning back.

"Wow, this place looks like a five-star hotel!" She set her tote purse on the computer desk and looked around the large room. The bed sat high off of the ground and had linens that looked softer than soft. The carpet was plush and clean, and there was a sofa to the far right of the room. Ramel had the fifty-inch television that hung on the wall turned off, and the large bathroom was on the other side of the room.

"That's what I thought too. Not too bad for eighty bucks a night. I could have done a lot worse."

There were a few seconds of silence. Awkward silence. Lina shrugged her shoulders and fell down into the computer chair. "Soooo . . ."

"So. Back at the coffee shop, you asked me how I knew about *them?*" he asked and went to the side of the bed where all of his travel bags were. From one he pulled out a laptop and went over to where Lina was sitting. Placing it in front of her, he opened it and clicked a few times. "Take a look."

She scooted closer to the desk so she could take a closer look at what was on the screen. There were pictures, lots of them. But not just any pictures. They were images of vampires, live vampires. Some were staked to trees, while others were chained in what looked like cellars. She clicked out of the images, and a document popped up; well, more like a journal.

"'New effective ways to use holy water to weaken the damned.'" Lina read the words out loud. "'Injection, blood dilution by drinking before'"—she paused and looked at Ramel with wide eyes—"'before hunting.' So you do hunt them?"

"For the past three years now. Ever since . . ." His voice trailed off, and he closed the laptop.

"Ever since what?"

Ramel turned his back to her and walked to the bed. He plopped down and stared at the lines on his hands for a second. "Ever since they took her from me."

Lina swallowed and contemplated whether she wanted to know who he was talking about. "Your girlfriend?"

"My sister," Ramel said. His voice had grown distant, and dark. "We were only a year apart; I was a year older than her. She was eighteen at the time they came. For some reason, they spared me. But they took her. I still remember the blood and her screams. They haunt my nightmares every night."

"That's why you started hunting?"

"I still remember what the vampire who took her looked like. His face is etched in my memory, and I will never stop until I find her."

"Have you gotten close?"

"That's what has brought me to North Carolina. I have tracked him. He goes by the name Rex, and I have reason to believe he is here."

Lina bit her lip. She hated thinking about the undead walking freely around her. It made her sick to her stomach.

"Is something wrong?" Ramel asked with concern in his voice after seeing the drastic change in her facial expression.

"It's just . . ." Lina paused. She cleared her throat and tried again. "Last year, I kind of had my own run-in with them. That's why you see me looking them up all the time. But, it's not to hunt them. It's to help me stay out of their way."

"Why?"

"I attended Billet University last school year and . . ."

"And?"

"There was a whole clan of them. They attended the school with us. They had their own frat house and everything."

"Wait. They attended school in the daytime?"

"Yes." Lina nodded.

"But how is that possible?"

"In some of the old texts I've read, it says that some vampires were given the knowledge to make rings that allow them to walk around in the daytime. Magic rings."

"Magic? Are you sure it wasn't sunscreen?"

"Sunscreen wears off," Lina answered. "I never saw any of them have to leave to reapply."

"Damn."

"Yeah," Lina said and felt her mind wander to Adirah. She didn't know why she was about to tell him everything; she just knew that she needed to get it out somehow. "They took a close friend of mine. She fell in love with their leader. So I guess that's not really taking, right? Not if she went willingly. This guy I was kind of seeing told me he would help me find out if they were all really vampires. Well, I know now, but I didn't know for sure at the time. We broke into their home, and one of them broke my wrist. Tried to kill me. Adirah saved me, though."

"And the boy with you?"

"Oh, him?" Lina chuckled. "It turns out that he was a vampire the whole time. A rival of theirs. He used me to infiltrate them and steal something."

"What did he want?"

"A small vial. I don't know what was in it, though. After he ditched me, so did Adirah. She ran to save her boyfriend and left me to fend for myself in a house full of hungry vampires."

"How did you get away, if you don't mind me asking?"

"They were all so distracted, I managed to slip out the back door. I didn't stop running until I was back inside of my dorm. But they knew me. They could find me if they wanted to. I left that day. Lost my scholarship, and my future went down the toilet."

"I'm sorry," Ramel said.

As she was talking, she didn't even hear or see him get up from the bed. He was now crouched in front of her, holding her hands sympathetically.

"Yeah." She gave him a sad smile. "Well, me too. Nothing I can do about it now."

"But there is."

"Like what? Hunt them down like you?" She expected him to laugh at her words. When he didn't, her eyes grew wide, and she pulled her hands away. "You can't be serious."

"Listen, it's not as hard as it sounds," he said taking her hands back again. "Also, I will be the first to tell you that once you have seen what goes bump in the night, you will never have peace of mind again. Unless . . ."

"Unless what?"

"Unless you do something about it."

"I don't know. I don't even know the first thing about hunting a deer."

"I'll show you. What do you have here to lose? Maybe this was your destiny. Imagine how many lives you'd save. Plus, this job gets kind of lonely. All the other hunters I know are pairs. They have each other's backs. So, what do you say, Lina?"

"I don't know, Ramel. I'm scared."

"I was too, on my first time. But I promise I won't let anything happen to you. I've kind of become an expert."

"An expert." Lina chuckled. "I'm talking to an expert vampire killer."

"Damn right," he said and shrugged. "If it makes you feel better, I can let you shadow me on a job just so you can see what it's all about."

No! Lina, tell this crazy-ass man no! Go back home to the safety of your apartment and forget that you even had this conversation at all!

Lina ignored the voice inside her head. It was what had gotten her into that situation in the first place. Maybe if she'd never gone into that frat house that day in the first place . . . But the past was the past. There was no changing it. Slowly, she nodded, and she saw Ramel's lips curl upward.

"Okay," Lina agreed. "But please don't get me killed."

Chapter 10

Thump! Thump! Thump!

Lina's heart was trying to escape through her chest. That night she only had plans to go home and catch up on her favorite reality television shows, but there she was, sitting in the parking lot of a nightclub in Ramel's all-black 2017 Jeep Wrangler. The clock read forty-five minutes past eleven and the scene she was watching looked pretty standard. Girls were trying to talk the bouncers into letting them in for free since they'd missed the deadline by fifteen minutes. Men were outside smoking cigarettes, eyeing the same girls trying to get in.

"My God," Lina said under her breath. "They might as well be naked!"

It was true that she'd grown out of wearing nothing but black, being that she knew for sure about the things that went bump in the night, but that didn't mean she was down with the skimpy look.

"You don't like their outfits?" Ramel smirked and cocked his head, as if he was trying to get a better angle of one of the girls.

"I mean, if you like women who dress like they want you to fuck them right then and there, hey," she said, shrugging, "more power to ya."

"I'm just kidding." Ramel chuckled. "I like my women a little more reserved."

That time he looked at her and, from the way his eyes spoke to her, she fidgeted in her seat. They were both wearing comfortable clothes, black, with a pair of boots to match. Lina suddenly felt like the neck of her hoodie was choking her and she was happy when Ramel finally looked away.

"So, did you think about how we are going to get in there?" she asked, changing the subject. "These types of nightclubs definitely have a dress code. We look like we're about to go in there and shoot up the place."

"We are." He reached to pop open the glove compartment, revealing two big black guns there. "About to shoot up the place, that is."

"Is that a pistol?"

"Glock 19s to be exact. With a few upgrades," he said pulling them out and handing her one. "The bullets inside are pure silver. When they hit their target, they will explode, giving off an ultraviolet light."

"What happens after that?"

"The vampire turns to ashes."

"Well, what happens if you miss?"

Ramel gave her a hard stare. "Don't miss."

"I don't know anything about aiming a gun. Let alone using one!"

"If a vampire is coming at you with its fangs out, you'll learn how to use it." Ramel turned the car back on and pulled the Jeep around to the back of the club, where the Dumpster was. "We're going to go in through there."

He pointed at a door that was clearly only supposed to be for employees. However, the closer Lina stared she could see that there was a rock holding the heavy door slightly ajar. She gripped the gun in her hand and was surprised at how it fit perfectly. She glanced down at it and breathed deeply. She could get out of the car and make a run for it, but just as that thought came to her mind, her wrist began to tingle. Ever since it healed, it always tingled at the most random times, reminding her exactly of what happened to her.

"I have a question," she said with her eyes still on the weapon.

"Shoot."

"You said these guns are special, and the bullets are special. That means somebody made them specifically for this purpose."

"Right."

"So exactly how many hunters are there in the world? And exactly how much money do they have? These weapons had to have cost a fortune. Not to mention that you don't have a job, but you're in a brand-new Jeep."

"If tonight goes well, I won't need to answer that question with words. I'll be able to show you. Come on. It's almost midnight."

He reached in the back seat of the Jeep and grabbed a backpack. Lina tucked the gun in the back of her pants and put her hoodie over it. By the time she got out of the vehicle, Ramel was already halfway to the door.

"Midnight?" Lina asked when she caught up to him.

"Yes. I heard rumors that midnight is when they feed in secret rooms. The guests are usually so drunk they don't know what's going on when they are escorted back. Wait." He had opened the door for Lina, but he put his hand out to stop her before she entered. "Always have your weapon ready when entering a battlefield."

"Right," Lina said wanting to slap herself. "Rookie mistake."

"A rookie mistake that could cost you your life."

His voice was so serious that Lina felt chills go down her back. Once inside, she took notice that they were in the kitchen of the club. A gust of cold air hit her, and the aroma of bleach filled her nostrils. The music on the dance floor was so loud she could sing along word for word with the music being played if she wanted to.

The coast looked to be clear, and Ramel motioned for her to follow him to a long hallway. There were two ways to go from the kitchen: one led to where the party was, and the other was the one they were going down. It was dark, and the only light was coming from the eerie red bulbs on the walls.

Lina began to feel anxious, so anxious that without even realizing it she fell far behind Ramel. She turned around in a circle to get a better look at the walls. They had strange pairs of claw marks on them, nail claw marks, as if someone had been dragged against their will down that hallway. The thing that made her sick to her stomach was that they were everywhere.

"Ramel, I—"

She turned back around to tell him to look at the walls, but he was nowhere to be found. She had a sinking feeling that maybe she'd been duped again. Narum's double cross entered her mind, and suddenly she remembered that she didn't even check Ramel's finger for a ring. He could have been a vampire the whole time, leading her into a trap.

"What are you doing back here?"

The gruff voice startled her, and she whipped around in the direction of the kitchen. There stood a tall, skinny man with short black hair. Physically he didn't look that much older than her, but his eyes . . . his eyes looked like they'd seen a world of hurt. There was a thirst in them that she recognized all too well.

"I got lost."

He chuckled and shook his head. "You don't look lost. You look like you're looking for something." He then moved so fast and, by the time Lina blinked, he was already behind her. "Or maybe, just maybe, you're looking for me?"

The gun! she thought.

"Gun, what gun?" the vampire said and grabbed her right hand. "Oh, this gun. Now, what were you going to do with this? Kill me? Hunter!"

The vampire ripped the gun from her hand and threw it before he whipped her around to face him. His long fingers wrapped around her neck and cut off her air. She watched him transform from a human to an all-out beast right in front of her. When his sharp white fangs lengthened, she knew that it was the end for her. The vampire hissed violently and reared its ugly head back in preparation to take a big chunk from Lina's exposed neck.

"Not today, you ugly motherfucker!"

Behind the vampire, Ramel had resurfaced and had his gun pointed at its head. He fired one time, and Lina flinched when the monster's head exploded into burnt ash. Its entire body turned into the same kind of ash and fell to the ground. Lina fell back, but Ramel caught her before she completely lost her balance. She caught her breath, suddenly realizing that this was for real. Whether she liked it or not, vampires existed, and it was either her or them, no matter what path she took.

"Thank you." She let go of Ramel and went to retrieve her gun. "Next time I won't be so easy. I thought you left me."

"I thought you were right behind me."

"I was, but then I got distracted by the marks on the wall," she said.

"I wouldn't leave you," he said with sincerity. "And I am definitely not a vampire."

She nodded and looked back at the claw marks on the walls. "It's like people, humans, were fighting for their lives."

"We are," he responded. "I found something. A door leading to the basement."

"Are we going down there?"

"Uh, hell no. That would be a suicide mission," he said. "Plus, they would sense us way before we attacked. This way."

She was confused, but she followed him. When they were in the large kitchen area, Ramel took the book bag off his shoulders and pulled out a vial. He took a swig from it and made a face at the taste of it.

"Here." He tried to hand it to her, but she hesitated. "It's a special concoction. The main ingredient is garlic. They won't be able to smell our blood or read our thoughts. In other words, we will be undetectable by them for a short while."

Lina thought back to how that vampire had read her thoughts and how invaded it made her feel. She grabbed the vial and took a swig from it. It was warm going down but, other than that, Lina didn't feel any different. Ramel took the vial and placed it back in his bag. He knew they wouldn't have much time before the vampires made their way upstairs to roam the streets at night.

Unbeknownst to Lina, not every vampire obtained a ring to be able to walk around during the day. There were the rogue vampires, the ones who didn't belong to a clan. They were more brutal, and they terrorized the streets the moment the last lick of light escaped the skies.

"This is the only way out from that way," Ramel told her, checking the clip of his gun.

"And they'll have to run right into us when the club lets out."

"Exactly."

"How many do you think there are?"

"Don't know," he said. "Could be a little, could be a lot. That's why I brought extra clips if we need them."

"I guess now we wai—"

A bloodcurdling scream behind her interrupted her statement. She heard panicked breaths and feet running toward the kitchen, followed by more screams. The night wasn't over yet, but the action started earlier than expected. Lina stayed behind Ramel, and they watched as a young woman ran into the kitchen. The makeup on her face was smeared due to the tears coming from her eyes, and her entire body was bloody. She looked around frantically, and her eyes found Ramel and Lina before they made an exit.

"Please, help me."

The whimper was barely out of her mouth when a vampire ran into the kitchen after her. It moved quickly, but Lina was shocked that she could see it. Before, their movements were like a blur to her; they were too quick. Now she had no problem keeping up with them with her eyes.

Bang!

Ramel wasted no time using his weapon on the monster, and he disintegrated it. He did the same thing when another came into the kitchen.

"Lina!" he called and glanced back at her. "They're coming! Get her and stay behind me."

"Get behind me," Lina said and grabbed the petrified girl. "I'm not going to let anything happen to you."

The kitchen was suddenly swarmed with vampires whose faces were covered in blood. It was apparent that they had just finished feeding but were upset their dessert had gotten away from them. They hissed with their long, sharp fangs out and they crouched low in battle positions. Lina, Ramel, and the girl the monsters wanted were surrounded, with a wall behind them.

"Three for the price of one," one of the female vampires said.

Lina was used to them being beautiful, but at that moment all she saw were the beasts they all were. Their brown skin glowed and as they moved and growled. The blood on their faces dripped to the floor.

The vampire who had spoken focused her attention on Lina. She stared into her eyes so intently, as if she was searching for something. When she didn't find it, she turned to Ramel and did the same thing, before she sneered.

"Hunters!"

At the sound of the word, the other vampires sneered even more ferociously.

"Yeah," Ramel said. "We're hunters, and it looks like you're going to be the second to die tonight."

Bang!

His bullet caught her right in the chest. She blew back as she disintegrated and the other vampires jumped to action. They came at Ramel with all that had.

Lina watched in awe as Ramel battled all of them. He was not only shooting them; he was fighting them. Actually fighting them. He moved with the same speed, meeting all of their attacks with blocks and knocking them back with powerful punches of his own. There were six vampires, and she knew that he would not be able to fend them off by himself.

It was like she felt something inside of her chest. It wasn't fear; it was more identical to hunger. Not a hunger for food, but a hunger to fight. That was the reason she wasn't shocked when a vampire attacked her, and she stepped out of the way with a speed she did not know she had.

"Agh!"

Her cry filled the air as she delivered an uppercut to the vampire's stomach, and followed through by twisting his arm behind his back and placing her gun on his temple. When she pulled the trigger, she didn't even wait before going toward a vampire trying to sneak up on Ramel.

"Behind you!" she yelled and ran so fast that the kitchen around her meshed together.

The vampire woman jumped toward Ramel, and Lina did the same, catching the vampire in midair with a powerful side kick.

"Bitch," Lina said as the vampire crashed into the cabinets behind her.

She put two bullets in her chest and continued fighting alongside Ramel until there were no more vampires standing. They fought like gladiators against a den full of lions. When Lina got into trouble, Ramel's guns got her out, and vice versa. They fought as a team, and one would be surprised to learn that this was their first time fighting together.

When all the opposition was defeated, the two of them stood in a kitchen full of dust, panting and trying to catch their breath.

"We need to get out of here," Ramel said, tucking his gun and turning his back to the long red hallway. "Let's get her to the hospit—"

"Ramel, look out!" she shouted and aimed her gun.

A final vampire stood behind Ramel calmly. He had appeared out of nowhere, and he slowly eyed the battle floor. He didn't have any blood on his face, nor was he transformed into his monster form. Lina knew he was a vampire because she saw the ring on his finger and she would recognize his face anywhere.

"Lina," he said in a voice that Lina remembered all too well.

Ramel moved out of the way and backed up to where Lina was. He glared at the young-looking vampire and wished that he hadn't put his weapon away. He looked to Lina, trying to understand how the monster knew her name, but her eyes were transfixed in front of her. She recognized the vampire, he could tell, and it was like she was frozen in place.

"Narum," she breathed.

Their eyes connected for a few moments and there were many unspoken words exchanged between the two of them. He was still as handsome as she remembered and he still dressed like a normal young adult. The last time Lina had seen him, he had led her into a suicide mission and left her to die. So why was it so hard to pull the trigger? Was it because she was just shocked? Or maybe it was because she often thought about the intimate moments they shared together. In her mind, she thought that the two of them would have started dating and even more would blossom from that. But he'd just been using her the whole time.

"In the flesh," he said and put his arms up in the air. "You're a hunter now, Lina?"

"I . . ."

"Well, I guess that part is a no-brainer. You have obviously just killed many of my brothers and sisters. I also can't read your thoughts."

"What are you doing here, Narum?"

"Isn't it obvious?" he asked. "This is the easiest place to come and grab a bite to eat. People like her." He nodded at the woman and flashed his fangs. "They come and basically hand themselves to my kind."

"You're a monster!"

"Was I a monster when I was between your legs?"

Lina wanted to pull the trigger so bad, but she couldn't. One shot and he would be ash, but it was like he had a hold on her.

"Lina, shoot it!"

"Oh, the disrespect," Narum taunted. "I am an it, and not a he? Typical hunter."

"Lina! Shoot!"

"She can't." Narum chuckled. "Because she doesn't want to."

"Lina!" Ramel yelled again, but he was starting to wonder if she could even hear her. "Fine. I'll kill this son of a bitch!"

He pulled his gun out to kill the smart-mouthed vampire but, before he could aim his gun, it was gone. The only thing he felt was a gust of wind, and he saw the exit door shutting once more. He turned back to Lina to chastise her, but he saw that she'd lowered her gun and her hand was shaking. He sighed and gently touched her arm.

"We need to go. There are probably all types of bodies in the basement of this place, and the feds will soon be looking for the first logical person to pin it on."

"Okay," Lina whispered and put her gun back on her waist.

"Hey," Ramel said and went to where the girl was kneeling in the corner of the kitchen. He knelt down as well so that he was eye to eye with her. "What is your name?"

"Brynn. Those things, those monsters, killed all of my friends. One of them tore my best friend's throat from her neck!"

"Well, Brynn, listen." Ramel had given this speech more times than he'd have liked. Each time his words got a little bit more heartless, but they were things that had to be said. "Life as you know it has changed forever. You survived, but your friends are never coming back. You now know about the evil that lurks at night. Leaving here and trying to pretend that nothing happened will only drive you crazy."

"So what am I supposed to do?"

Ramel reached in his pocket and pulled out a card. "Take a day or two to yourself. If you cannot shake your thoughts, or feel that you need to do something about what you've seen tonight, call me."

He stood and started in the direction of the red hallway. He knew there was one last thing he needed to do. "Lina, go to the car."

"What are you doing?"

"Leaving the hunter's mark," he said, reloading his gun and cocking it. "And making sure that they didn't turn any of their victims tonight."

Chapter 11

Back at the Malum Camp

Calum's moans filled the air as she allowed the love of her life to take her from behind. No matter how many times they made love, she simply could not get enough. She could tell that Talum needed to let off some frustration, and inside of her was the best place to do so. She loved submitting to him sexually and letting him use her body as a sense of release. It made her feel good to know that he needed her.

"Oh, Talum," she cried feeling her fangs grow. She bit down hard on the pillow her arms and head were resting on, tearing a big hole in it. "Fuck me, baby! I need it."

"You need it?" His voice came out low and gruff.

"Yes. Please don't stop!"

"I don't want to, Calum." His voice turned into a moan in the middle of his statement. "I don't want to, but you know what you do to me!"

Calum bucked her wide hips backward, matching him for every thrust. She knew that he couldn't handle it when she did that, but she felt her climax coming around the corner and would do anything to get it faster. They sexed each other harder and faster until finally, they both reached their finish lines. Talum jerked and fell on top of Calum, holding her tightly at the waist. They both shouted out in unison until their orgasms had passed, leaving them breathless.

It was the most amazing feeling, being able to lie with the one you loved. After their last fight with Kesh and Adirah, Calum had come to cherish those moments even more. She realized that she'd forgotten she was only immortal as far as age, but she could still be killed.

Talum released himself from her and rolled over on his back so that Calum could lay her head on his chest. Even though she had just put it down on him so good that any ill thought should have been gone from his mind, she knew that something was still bothering him. She could sense it. There was once a time long ago when the two of them shared thoughts, but now they both kept what was on their minds to themselves.

"What is wrong with you, Talum?" she asked and, when he took a breath to speak, she cut him off. "And do not lie to me and say, 'Nothing.' Like I am not the same person who has spent years of her endless life with you. Don't insult me."

Talum sighed and kissed Calum on the forehead. He knew the questions would start happening sooner or later. He'd just been buying himself time since Calum had been so in tune with her training. The truth was, there was something bothering him. It was a feeling: a feeling that wouldn't allow him to ignore it no matter how hard he tried to. If he could describe the feeling in color, it would be a bright and bold red.

"I feel something."

"Something like what?"

"Evil."

"Evil?"

"Yes. Evil. Something is coming," he said. "Something that none of us will be able to stop."

"What do you mean?"

"I don't know." He sighed. "It's in the back of my mind and has been for some time now. It is . . . unsettling."

"The Sefu?"

Talum shook his head. That was the reason he did not want to say anything. He knew Calum wouldn't understand. When he'd found her, she was newly turned and running from witches and

Lykans. Even when he took her under his wing, he kept her shielded from the real world of monsters out there. She did not know about the great wars fought between vampires and Lykans. She, just like many of the other vampires, thought they were just stories. He, however, had always been interested in the ways and history of vampires. Ever since he'd been turned by Kesh, he wanted to know and be in tune with exactly what he was. He read in ancient textbooks about the War of the Ancients. It was the most brutal war in the history of their kind, and they almost lost.

The difference between vampires and Lykans was that vampires were okay with coexisting with humans. Granted, they were also vampires' food. One cannot blame the nature of the beast. One can only be patient at taming its thirst. It seemed as if they were going more in the direction of blood harvesting and owning blood banks, simply because the hunters of that day and age were becoming more powerful. Either way, vampires never wanted to rule the world; they were content with running the underworld.

Lykans, on the other hand, wanted both worlds. They were considered to be vampires' greatest enemy because they not only wanted to rule both worlds, they wanted to be the dominant race of monsters. Lately, there was a passage from one of the books Talum had read that would not leave his mind: "Three of the Ancient Lykans were laid to rest, while the other two waited patiently for their time to rule over the world. When they have arisen, only the most powerful of creatures will feel their presence."

Talum hoped that this wasn't the presence he'd been feeling. But with everything going on at that point, including Adirah giving birth to the first vampire baby, there was no telling what would happen next.

Suddenly a thought entered his mind and made him sit straight up in the bed.

"Talum, what is it?"

He didn't answer her. Jumping out of bed, he put on the red silk pajama pants that lay on the side of the bed. He didn't see her frantically throwing on her robe behind him as he jetted out of their room and ran down the long hall to the library.

"It's here. It has to be here! I would not have left it behind."

He rummaged through the many tall bookshelves in hopes of finding what he was looking for. It took a while, but finally, his hands lay on the small black book that he was looking for.

"Here it is," he whispered and opened the book. "Now where is that passage?"

He flipped the gold, thin pages in the book until he came across one that was labeled "The Golden Child."

There will be one born to vampire who will be able to walk in the daylight and drink the blood of mortals at his own will. He is one who all vampirekind must protect with their most precious of life, for his is more important. For his blood has the power to turn the darkest inhuman of hearts mortal again.

He was so entrapped in the passage that he didn't even feel Calum come up behind him. She read the words over his shoulder and clenched her teeth, forcing her jaw into a straight line.

"Do you think . . . Do you think it's talking about Adirah's baby?"

His silence did not comfort her; it confirmed her thoughts. She still didn't understand what all was going on but, by the stricken look on Talum's face, it couldn't be good. Gently, she closed the book in his hands. "Talum. What does it mean?"

"It means the end for us all very well may be near. Darkness is coming."

Calum tried to find words, but she couldn't. The way his statement came out clutched her cold heart in a way that made it hard for her to breathe. The only thing that she was able to do was hold on to Talum's arm. He took notice of the shift in the air and pulled her in for a deep embrace.

A throat clearing at the entrance of the library interrupted their moment. "Sire, I wish to speak to you for a moment if that is not a problem."

Talum looked up and was looking into the eyes of one of his soldiers, Narum. Before, the two had been at odds, but Talum soon realized that Narum was the type of vampire who would do anything for his clan. He risked his life to bring Talum the magical elixir that Kesh held. If only Talum hadn't instantly been so hard on him, he would still have the potion.

Talum nodded at Narum and kissed Calum on her forehead. "I will be back to bed soon, my queen."

Of course, Calum wanted to stay and see what they were going to discuss, but she would not stay anywhere she was not wanted. "Narum," she said as she passed.

"My queen," Narum said giving a respectful bow. When she was gone, he stepped into the library and cleared his throat again. "I do apologize for barging in so suddenly."

"I assume it is only because you have brought me news," Talum stated.

"Of course, my king. It is about the human girl."

"You have found her?"

"Yes."

"I hope you killed her before she was picked up by—"

"Hunters? Too late." Narum swallowed as he could tell the news did not make his king happy.

"How do you know of this information?"

"I saw it with my own eyes. She was with one of their most skilled hunters."

"Ramel?"

"Yes. They destroyed a whole fleet of new vampires."

"Just the two of them you say?"

"Yes, sir, just the two of them."

"Then she is strong."

"Not strong yet; fearless. She will have a vendetta against both the Sefu and the Malum. I worry that I may be at fault for this."

Talum stared at Narum for a few moments. He had been one of the people Talum had turned by accident long ago in his thirst. In a sense, the way that Narum worked overtime to gain Talum's approval was equivalent to a son trying to earn his father's approval. Talum wanted to place blame somewhere, but he knew that he could only place it on himself.

A year ago, he was a completely different kind of vampire: ruthless and without mercy. Ever since he left the Sefu so long ago, it was like he was on a journey to find something, something that he would never be able to find or have again: his humanity. That birthed the anger inside of him. It fueled the beast he never wanted to be. Once he was defeated by Kesh, it did something completely opposite of what it had done to Adirah. He was humbled.

"I cannot hold you at fault for taking a risk for your people. For me. I only wish that the human girl would have been dealt with at the time of the infiltration." He paused and gave Narum a knowing look. "Or before you got involved with her. Other than the fact that she is now affiliated with the ones who want us extinct, will there be any other problems? Or entanglements?"

"No, my king," Narum answered quickly. "She was nothing. It will stay that way."

"Okay," Talum said and sat down in one of the chairs in the library. "And about the vampires who were killed . . ."

"No worries, sire. We will make up for the lost instantly."

"No." Talum shook his head and waved his hand. "These new vampires are too reckless. The irony is, if we hope to survive much longer we do not need added numbers. I decree that it is now unlawful to create a new vampire without the approval of the king."

"Or what, sire?"

"Or they will be banished and released from this camp, in the daytime, with no rings."

Narum swallowed. "When should this be effective?"

"Immediately. Now leave me."

Narum did as he was told and shut the door to the library behind him. He too had much to think about, mainly about why Lina didn't pull the trigger on the gun when she had an open shot. He didn't think that she would be an issue, especially not that she was a hunter. But the more he thought about it he couldn't help but question a few things.

He couldn't lie and say that he hadn't thought about her since the day he left her at the Sefu camp. He didn't want it to be that way, but his loyalty was to his people. She would never have understood. If she knew at the time what he really was, he wouldn't have gotten that far with her in the first place. Would he have?

Chapter 12

Kesh didn't have much time to prepare for his meeting with the Malum. He contemplated the best way to go about doing the task, and he finally decided the best route would be the window.

"The window?" Adirah raised her eyebrow at him. Her eyes were on the side of his face. She'd been watching him for some time and knew that he was contemplating a plan. When he sent the first smile her way and finally told her what he was thinking she stared in disbelief. "That's the plan, Kesh? The window?"

"Yes." Kesh grinned at her. "We're going to have to sneak in."

"We're going to have Malum all over us."

"Either way we're going to have Malum all over us. I opt for the one that's going to buy us a little more time."

"Absolutely not!" Adirah exclaimed when he told her the plan. "They'll be all over us before we even find Talum's bedchamber."

"That's only if we decide to go through the front door," Kesh told her as he played with baby Adis in their large chamber. "And that's also only if we do not know where the chambers are to begin with."

Adirah rested her eyes on her son's face. His eyes smiled almost as big as his lips as his dad threw him high into the sky and caught him when he came back down. The Ancients had accommodated their stay with comfy living arrangements, better than any Adirah had ever experienced in her life. Their chambers were the same size as a two-bedroom apartment, only everything was open. Adirah had to admit she felt like royalty when she walked on the lion skin carpet, or when she lay her head on the Egyptian cotton pillows on the bed.

It saddened her to know that she would have to leave her son behind, but she knew there was no other way. She couldn't turn a blind eye knowing what was going on around her. It was planned that Adis would stay back with Dena, who promised to protect him with her life. Adirah vowed to make it back to her son, but it looked as if Kesh was doing everything in his power to ensure that wasn't going to happen.

"There is no other way," Kesh reasoned.

"There is always another way."

"Was there another way when I lay dying?"

Adirah was quiet. Her becoming a vampire was never part of the plan, and Kesh definitely didn't want that life for her. There was the constant thirst, but mostly he couldn't bear the thought of her being unhappy with him for a lifetime. Vila had tricked her into doing the deed that he was most against in hopes that he would fall out of love with her. What no one seemed to understand was that he did not love her for her humanity; he loved her for her.

"That's different, Kesh, and you know it."

"No, it's very much the same."

"Enlighten me."

"Sometimes we have to do things we don't want to do for the greater good of our kind." Kesh was silent for a few moments. He set Adis on the ground and let him crawl off to one of the many toys Lira had lavished on him. "Do you regret this?"

Adirah was taken aback by his question and her brow formed into a straight line. She could tell by his solemn expression that he'd asked it in all seriousness. Her first reaction was to snap at him, but she knew that wasn't what he needed right then. She crawled to where he sat on the floor and straddled him. She placed a soft palm on his right cheek and kissed him gently on his lips.

"Vampire or human, I couldn't imagine living without you," she told him. "Rain, sleet, or snow, I will be by your side. So, I guess it's good that I am a vampire now; you don't have to worry too much about defending me. I can protect you now too. If this is truly the only way that you think will work, I'm with you. Do you trust me, Kesh?"

"Yes."

"Then don't ever ask me that question again."

They exchanged a look of understanding, and she leaned in for a kiss. When their lips touched that time, Adirah detected hesitation. She kissed him again, but he hesitated once more. "There's something else on your mind?"

"Yes."

"What is it?"

"Now that we are here with the Ancients, there is something that I need to tell you. It's something about our pasts. Something that I hope does not change the way you feel about me."

"Just tell me. There's nothing that you can tell me that could ever change the way I feel about you."

"Don't make promises that you cannot keep, my love."

"Kesh, you're scaring me. Say whatever it is so we can move past it."

The look in his eyes right then was one she'd never seen. It was deeper than sorrow and not close enough to fear. It was unreadable.

"Kesh . . ."

"It might have been written in the stars for our paths to cross."

"What? What do you mean?"

"Adie. I'm talking about Adie."

"Well, what about Adie? The fact that she turned you?"

"No, I'm talking about before she turned me."

"Okay, Kesh. This isn't making any kind of sense to me."

"Before she turned me, she was very special to me. I cared about her deeply, and when she died, it consumed me."

"You were . . ." Adirah's forehead crinkled up as she suddenly realized what he was trying to tell her. "Kesh, were you in love with Adie?"

"Yes, I was in love with her before she died. And many years after."

It felt like all the breath in Adirah's chest had left her for dead. She sat on Kesh's lap, frozen in shock replaying his words in her mind. Surely, he hadn't said what she thought he did. He was in love with Adie? Her great ancestor? She suddenly had no urge to touch him any longer, let alone be in his presence. Kesh tried to grab her arm so that she would not move, but she snatched away from him. She couldn't believe what he had just told her. She stood up and turned her back to him, trying to find her words.

"Do I remind you of her?" Her voice was a raspy whisper. "Is that why you fell in love with me?"

"No, Adirah."

"How long have you known?"

"Not too long."

"How long have you known!" She tried to, but she was not able to mask the shake in her voice. The tears had snuck up on her and were making a warm path down her face.

"Not too long after your accident last year. It was after I fell in love with you. I always wondered why I was so drawn to you, but then the pieces began fitting together."

"On what? That I reminded you of the woman you're actually in love with?"

"No, my queen. That this is fate! Don't you see?"

Adirah scooped Adis into her arms and shot piercing glares back toward Kesh. Her heart ached something vicious, and it was not a feeling that words could fix. Fate? How could she find comfort in fate when she was his choice number two?

"See what, your lies? The other vampires thought you loved me for my humanity. But they were wrong, isn't that right? You love me because it is Adie's blood that runs through my veins!"

"That's not true, Adirah. Please don't think like that."

At that point, Kesh had gotten to his feet too, but he didn't dare go near her. Although the only thing he wanted to do was hold her in his arms and reassure her, he knew that would not be a very smart move. Still, the look of hurt on her face made him feel a despair in his stomach that he was trying to avoid. That was the reason he danced around telling her for so long, but being so close to Dena he knew that he'd better tell her or someone else would.

"I thought I was special to you."

"You are, Dira," Kesh said with a plea in his voice. "I love you with every part of me. Don't you understand? I love you, Adirah."

"But I'm not the love of your life, am I?"

To that, Kesh was quiet. He could not lie to her; he refused to, even if the payment for his truth was to watch the tears pour seamlessly from her eyes. He hated seeing her that way and tried to take a step toward her, but she backed away from him.

"Stay away from me! Just stay the hell away from me!"

Her shouts hurt his heart more than his ears. She ran from the room, and he let her go. He deserved her anger and did not want to ignite it any more than it had been already. He sighed deeply and hung his head in defeat.

"I knew you hadn't told her."

The voice caught Kesh off guard, but he knew who it was. "I never thought I would have to."

Dena stared at Kesh with a glassy expression before her eyes softened. "You look miserable. Take a walk on the grounds with me."

When Kesh hesitated, she waved her hand slightly in the air and used her power to nudge his back, forcing him to take a step forward. "Come on. I don't intend to bite you."

There was no telling where Adirah had gone to in the large castle, and he figured she wouldn't be showing her face for a while. Also, Dena had the power to make Kesh float to wherever she wanted him to go, so why not go willingly?

As he walked alongside her, he learned many secret passages in the castle to get to the lowest level of the castle. When they were finally outside, the pair walked in silence for a few minutes. They passed many other curious vampires outside enjoying time together. As they passed, many of them broke out into a fit of whispers. If they caught Kesh's eyes, they would instantly look away.

"I guess they aren't too pleased with my presence here."

"Who, them?" Dena asked. "No. Every vampire in the world is welcome here."

"Then why does it seem like they fear to look me in the eye?"

"Your name precedes you, my dear Kesh. Do you not know who you are?"

"Yes, I am king of the Sefu."

Dena chuckled and shook her head. She raised her eyebrow at him as he walked beside her. The concentrated look on his face let her know that his mind was elsewhere, but she needed him there and to understand who he was fully.

"No. You are Kesh. King of *all* vampires."

"All vampires?"

"Yes." Dena nodded. "Aside from us Ancients, you are the strongest vampire alive. You have only slightly tapped into the power that Adie passed to you."

"What kind of power?"

"You, Kesh, have every power of an Ancient in you. The only difference is that the normal things that can kill a vampire can still kill you too. It would just take a little longer."

She winked at him, and he stopped walking. He was trying to take in all that she had said.

King of all vampires?

"Wait!" Kesh jogged to catch up to her, and she stopped. "If what you are saying is true, why haven't I tapped into the powers yet?"

"Because, just like us, you need to be trained."

"When will my training start?" His voice was too eager, and Dena noticed it.

"Once you come back with both clans in tow, and once my niece forgives you."

"One of those, I can definitely do."

"And the other?"

Kesh's shoulders slumped slightly. "I don't know how to bring her back."

"You don't believe that she still loves you?"

"The way she looked at me—"

"She still loves you," Dena interrupted in a matter-of-fact tone.

"How do you know?"

"Because if she didn't she would have sent you flying across the room, but she didn't."

Kesh didn't know why, but he found himself laughing. He and Dena smiled at each other before continuing their walk.

"But will she ever forgive me?"

"Give her some time," Dena said. "Given we survive what's to come, she'll come around. Adie was special to all of us. She was our heart. Unlike the rest of us, she always had a soft spot for the humans. She never wanted to harm them, and she would prefer to drink from an animal if she could help it. When she abandoned us to fight a war for them, I was so angry at her. I—"

"You what?"

"I said some things that I wish I could take back. So I apologized, right before she left the castle for the last time, in hopes that she would stay. But she still declined. She said she couldn't stay here with us."

"Why?"

"Because after all the boy toys she'd had in life, she messed around and fell in love." Dena touched his chin ever so softly. "With you. A mortal boy back then. She gave her life for you, Kesh. At the time I didn't understand, but now I do. After spending time with Adirah and baby Adis, I would die for them. More than once. The difference between the two loves is that Adie is gone. Cherish her memory, but release the hold that you have on it. Because Adirah is here. Whether Adie knew what she was doing back then or not, she let you go a long time ago. It's time you do the same."

"I don't know how to let her go. I've tried, but—"

"Too many unanswered questions?"

"Yes. I feel as if this weight on my heart is not fair to Adirah. But I do not know how to free myself from it."

"What do you think will help you move on?"

"I don't know." Kesh's shoulders sank for a moment. He thought of Adie's beautiful face and her graceful nature. He wondered if she'd always been the person he knew. "What was she like? Before she came to North Carolina?"

"Adie was a handful, I'll tell you that." Dena chuckled.

"How old were you when Dracula turned you?"

"I was twenty-five, and Adie was twenty-three. Dracula chose when it was time to turn us into his soldiers, but he gave us a choice. He'd grown fond of us over the years, especially Adie."

"What do you mean?"

"See for yourself."

Dena placed two fingers on Kesh's forehead and sent him back in time.

The two girls' giggles filled the grassy clearing as they ran side by side together. There was something about feeling the earth between their toes and looking up at the night sky that always made them happy. They were playing a game, one of the many nameless games they played, to see who could collect the most beautiful flowers.

The trick was that it was dark, so sometimes they thought they were plucking a beautiful flower, but in actuality, it would be a weed.

"Adie, look!" ten-year-old Dena said to her eight-year-old sister. "Fireflies!"

Adie already had spotted them. They both forgot about their flower hunt and dropped the ones in their arms to the ground. They danced around in a circle, and it was like the fireflies were dancing with them. Their long dresses twirled in the light wind of the night, and they sang a song that they made up long before.

"Sisters forever, sisters together. You and me! A bond never broken, Dena and Adie!"

Dena grabbed Adie by the hand, and the two of them ran around and around as fast as they could before collapsing in the soft grass. Adie scooted close to her sister and rested her head on her arm, and their eyes fell on the stars.

"What do you think is up there?"

"Heaven," Dena answered with a smile. "It's so beautiful, the only answer can be heaven. That's why I'm not scared to die."

"That's because you're crazy, sister. "

"Maybe." Dena kissed Adie on the forehead. "Your crazy sister Dena."

"I wouldn't have it any other way," Adie said and then sighed suddenly. "I'm afraid to die."

"Why, sister?

"Because even though the stars are beautiful, there are so many beautiful things down here too. What if there aren't any flowers in heaven?"

"I'm sure there are more beautiful flowers there than there are down here," Dena assured her. "And I'm sure there are also as many sweet cakes as you can eat!"

"Mmm." Adie smiled at the thought of a warm apple pastry melting on her tongue. "I would like that a lot!"

"I know you would."

The two lay there for as long as they could stand the itchy grass, which was a long time. When finally Dena felt that their mother would be worried about them, she sat up and pulled Adie to her feet as well.

"Mother is going to have a fit if she sees all this grass and dirt in our hair. Here." Dena knelt down so that Adie could see the top of her pinned-up bun. "Help me and I will help you."

"Fair."

Adie picked off every small stick and piece of grass that had latched on to Dena's curls. When they were all gone she bent her head down so that Dena could do the same for her. Dena was right: if their mother knew that they were *rolling around in the dirt again, she would have both of their hides for dinner.*

Dena grabbed Adie's hand once she was all finished and prepared to head back to their small cottage when she heard the sound of a branch snapping in the distance. She whipped her head to where the sound came from, fearful that a wild animal had heard them playing. Her eyes skimmed the edge of the forest that she and Adie were not allowed to enter when, finally, her eyes set on something.

What she'd heard was not a wild animal. With the moon as her only light, she was not able to make out a face, but she was positive that there was a tall man standing beside a group of tall bushes.

"Do you see him, Dena?" Adie whispered and gripped her sister's arm tight.

"Yes," Dena whispered back. Her heart had either slowed or stopped completely, and she was frozen in place. She wanted to take Adie and run to their cottage, but she was too frightened to do even that. If she screamed, she was certain that her father would be able to hear her, yet her mouth refused to move. It was almost as if she were in a trance of some kind; and, when she blinked, the man was gone. Still, something told her that they were not alone.

That's when she felt it: his breath on the back of her neck. She jumped and spun around. Sure enough, there he was, up close and standing with his hands behind his back.

He was probably the most handsome man Dena had ever seen, with his perfect jaw structure and high cheekbones. His skin was the color of smooth cocoa and, up close, Dena could tell that his eyes were a different color than any she had ever seen before. They were amber and looked as if they were looking right into her soul.

"How did you get over here so quickly?" she asked, not understanding what had just happened. "That's impossible."

"I thought I would be a gentleman and come grab these for you since you dropped them."

From behind his back, he presented the flowers that the girls had dropped, only before he handed them to the girls he waved his hand over them once. The girls watched in disbelief as the flowers transformed from lilies and daisies to roses right before their eyes. They were the prettiest roses they'd ever seen. They were as red as the blood in their veins, and the stems were greener than the healthiest grass. Adie must have forgotten that the man was a complete stranger, because she pulled away from her sister and stepped forward to grab the flowers from the man's hand.

"Adie!" Dena tried to grab her sister, but it was too late.

"Don't worry," he said. "If I wanted to hurt you, then you would already be in pain."

He split the dozen roses in his hands and gave six to Adie and held out the other six to Dena. Reluctantly, she took the roses and instinctively put them to her nose. She inhaled them and gasped at their scent. "They smell like peaches!"

"Mine smell like my favorite apple pastry!" Adie said in awe as she inhaled the smell of her flowers. "But, mister, how did you do that?"

"Magic!" he said and waved his hands in the air again for theatrics.

"Who are you anyways?" Dena asked.

"My name is not important to you yet. But, in due time, you will know who I am."

"Why are you talking so weird?"

"Adie!"

"What? I don't even know what 'in due time' means!"

The man chuckled at the girls' exchange before running a smooth hand down Adie's cheek. He smiled down at her, and she found herself smiling back up at him.

"Adie, dear Adie. I knew I always liked you."

Adie opened her mouth to say something but a voice that both she and Dena recognized interrupted her. "Dena! Adie! Supper is ready!"

"Mother!" both girls whispered in unison.

If she caught them talking to a strange man in the night, she would be madder than if she found grass and sticks in their hair. Dena looked from the man, who gave her a slow smile before waving his fingers, to her mother slowly approaching with a lantern candle. She turned back to the man to tell him that they had to go, and she sucked her teeth with wide eyes.

"He's gone," Adie told her. "He moved really fast, Dena. Faster than anything I've ever seen! I can't wait to tell Mother and Father."

"No!" Dena told her as her mother got into hearing range. "You must not say a word about the man to them. They will worry."

"Where have you two been hiding? I've been looking for you for five minutes!"

Their mother, Ivory, put her hand on her hip and examined the girls top to bottom as if she was looking for something but didn't know what it was. The girls were stuck for a moment, not knowing what to say.

Dena finally cleared her throat and gave her mother the most believable smile that she could muster. "We just were running after fireflies," Dena said, telling half of the truth.

"What's this you have there? Are you hiding something?"

"No!" Dena spat out before she realized her mother was asking about the flowers she'd subconsciously placed behind her back. "Oh, these? Adie and I picked them earlier."

"Is that true, Adie?"

"Yes. Tell her, Adie." Dena's eyes prompted Adie to say something, and she saw the thick line appear on her little sister's forehead. It always came when Adie was about to do something that she did not want to do. Dena felt horrible for asking her to lie to their mother, but there was no other way. The last thing Dena wanted was to go to sleep with a raw bottom. Still, if Adie didn't say something quick, their mother would know Dena was lying.

"Yes, Mother," Adie finally said. "We found a rosebush with only twelve roses. We picked them because they would look so beautiful on the dining room table. Don't you think?"

She held hers out, and her mother grabbed them. The first thing she did was put them to her nose and inhale. She made a stale face and shook her head. "They're beautiful, but they smell worse than manure." Ivory gagged again, and the girls exchanged a look of wonder. "Come on, let's not keep your father waiting any

*longer. He did not want to begin eating his stew
without you girls."*

*The girls followed their mother back to their
cottage and Dena couldn't help but look back at
the edge of the forest. She didn't have to search
hard for what she was looking for, because just
as she was about to be out of sight, she saw the
pair of amber eyes looking back at her.*

"Was that . . ." Kesh began when Dena brought
him back.

"Dracula? Yes. He looks different than what
you expected, doesn't he?"

"Yes. I thought he would look more sinister."

"Do not let his looks fool you. He is as sinister
as the stories say."

"Then why didn't he kill you and Adie? You
were only two small children. Seems like the
easiest of any prey."

"You did not allow me to finish. He is as sinister as the stories say, but Dracula is a force who
acts on his own accord. He had other plans for
Adie and me. Plans that we had no clue of until
later in life."

"I assume that you are going to show me now?"

Dena smiled and put her two fingers back on
Kesh's forehead. "Precisely."

*Years had gone by, and soon the girls forgot
all about the strange man. They grew up into*

the most beautiful women and, when their mother died, their father sent them to America. Everything was so different from Cameroon, and the way they were treated by those with lighter skin appalled them. It took a while to adjust, but eventually, the girls found their footing in society.

Dena got a job at a fabric company, sewing materials together the way her mother had taught her, while Adie worked at home baking her favorite pastries for people around the small town they lived in. They didn't have much, but they had each other, and that was always just enough for them.

Often, Dena was the last worker of the night. She enjoyed being able to come to work and start something fresh versus having to finish something from the day before. One night, after she finished the quilt for Mrs. Hinson down the road, she decided that it was time to go home. It was almost nine o'clock, and she was certain that Adie had something good cooking on the stove. She grabbed her petticoat and the lock-up keys so that she could be on her way. After locking the door, she began the five-minute walk to her home.

That night it was chilly, so she tucked her ears behind her collar and put her hands in

*her pockets to keep them warm. She wished
she would have worn her hair down that day;
at least the thickness of it would have kept
the tips of her ears from being nipped. She
was alone outside, as she often was when
she walked home. Everyone in the neighborhood surrounding the shop was in their homes,
enjoying their meals with their families. She
smiled to herself wondering what crazy story
Adie would have for her that night.*

*She'd only gotten about one hundred feet
from the shop when she heard footsteps behind
her. She didn't turn around to see who they
belonged to; she just sped up her pace. Hopefully
whoever it was would either go right past her
or enter one of the houses she'd walked by. No
such luck. A rough hand grabbed her arm and
whipped her around.*

*"Is this the pretty nigger girl you've been
telling me about, Rolland?"*

*Alarmed, Dena snatched away and stepped
backward from the man who had grabbed her
arm. She'd never seen him a day in her life and
didn't know why he thought that it was okay to
grab her the way that he had. He had a head
full of red hair, with a red beard to match. He
had to have been years older than her, and
she hated the way his eyes ran over her body*

like she was a piece of meat. He was with two other men, one of whom Dena recognized as the nephew of the owner of the shop she worked in. She'd noticed Rolland giving her the eye a few times, but she never would have pegged him as the type of man who would plot on her. Then again, she was told the moment she stepped into America never to trust a white devil.

"Yeah, that's her, Joe. Pretty as pie, isn't she?"

Joe whistled his answer and licked his lips at Dena. For every backward step she took, he took one forward.

"Don't ever touch me again," she snapped and glared at him. "That is not how you treat a lady."

"I would never grab a lady like that." He grinned sneakily. "But you aren't a lady, are you?"

"What do you want?"

"I want something that you got, of course," Joe said and rubbed his hand on his crotch. "I got an itch that I need you to scratch. Boy, you have some nice lips."

"Go to hell!" Dena shouted and spat at his feet. "I wouldn't let you touch me if you were the last man on earth!"

"Who said anything about you letting us?"

On his signal, the other two men stepped forward and grabbed Dena, covering her mouth before she could scream. She fought as hard as she could, but it was no use. They were too strong. She did, however, manage to scratch Rolland good in the face. He gave her a brutal backhand to hers in return. Her head snapped back, and the blood instantly began trickling out of her nose. Her ears rang loudly, and the world around her was a blur as they dragged her out of the street.

"There's an alley behind that old butcher's market over there!"

When they got her to the alley, out of the eyesight of any onlookers, they dropped her by a couple of metal trashcans.

"This is where we're going to put you when we're done with ya," Rolland sneered. "You niggers think you can just move here and everything is going to be all peaches. My uncle is too nice to your kind. Well, I'm from the South, and the only peaches we like are the ones under your skirt."

"I can't wait to see what she looks like underneath these clothes," Joe said. "Hey! Don't let any blood get on that coat and dress. My wife loves that color blue."

"You men should be ashamed of yourselves," she whispered. "You will all rot in hell."

"Maybe," Joe said, unzipping his pants after Rolland and the other man hiked her skirt up and removed her underclothes. "But not before you, bitch!"

Dena clenched her eyes shut, not believing what was happening. She didn't even get the chance to tell Adie that she loved her one last time, or good-bye for that matter. Dena held in her tears, not wanting to give them the satisfaction of seeing her cry. She swallowed her sobs back and said a silent prayer, accepting her fate.

Suddenly, she felt the hands that were on her just go away, and that was followed by a few grunts and thuds. In front of her, she heard the sound of someone gurgling, but she was too frightened to open her eyes. She counted to ten, and by the last number, all of the sounds around her had stopped. Slowly, she opened her eyes, and she had to throw her hands over her mouth to keep from screaming.

Laid out in front of her with a hole missing from his neck was Joe. His eyes were frozen open in shock, and she knew he was dead. Behind her, Rolland and the other man she did not know were sprawled out on their stomachs in awkward positions. Pools of blood leaked from under them and onto the concrete *ground of that alley. Her legs buckled as she tried to stand up. She didn't think she would be able to walk, but she knew she had to get out of there. Three dead white men couldn't mean her any good.*

"Do not be afraid, my dear Dena."

The voice shook her. It was one that she vaguely remembered, one that she only heard rarely in her dreams. Her head whipped left and right trying to find the source of it. That was when her eyes landed on those the color of amber. The memories of that night she and Adie were picking flowers and catching fireflies plagued her mind. Fear struck her heart, not because of the blood dripping from his skin, but because he looked exactly the same as he did in her memories. He hadn't aged a single day.

"Stay away from me," she whispered and held her hand out as if to keep him at bay. "Leave me be. You killed them."

"Dena, do not be scared of me. I only want to protect you. These men were about to do a very bad thing to you. They deserved a death worse than this."

Dena looked again to the bodies of the men who had attempted to take her virginity, and she could not deny that she felt no sympathy for them. They were going to cause her a shame above all shames and just leave her body to rot. Was that what America was about? She turned her attention back to the man and noticed that the blood was completely gone from his face. He'd taken a few steps closer to her, out of the shadows. Still, he stayed far enough away so as not to feel like a threat to her.

"Who are you?"

"Ahh," he said placing a finger in the air. "Is that the right question to ask?"

"What are you?" Dena tried again.

"Ding, ding, ding. Now that would be the correct answer. What do you think I am?"

"A monster."

"I have been called that many times, especially when people see my true nature."

"Your true nature?"

"Yes," he said. "They usually run away screaming."

Without warning, he transformed quickly in front of her, revealing his hideous face, long fangs, bulky muscles, and sharp claws. Dena gasped and screamed loudly. Her feet couldn't move quick enough as she ran out of the alley and toward her home.

"Like that." He chuckled, transforming back to his human form.

Dena ran like a madwoman until she reached her front door. She banged on it and feverishly checked behind her to see if she had been followed. It took Adie all of ten seconds to come to the door, but to Dena, it felt like a lifetime. She fell into her sister's arms, and Adie instantly knew something was wrong.

"Dena, what's going on? What happened to your face?"

"Mr. Alfred's nephew and his friends tried to force themselves on me," Dena gasped.

"What!" Adie made like she was about to go outside but Dena pulled her back and slammed the door shut.

"No!"

"Dena, some men tried to hurt you! Just because we have color on our skin does not make it right for people to assault you! I'm going to get help." Adie snatched away and made to open the door again.

"They're dead."

"They're what?" Adie shut the door and turned to her sister. "What did you say?"

"They're dead. In the alley by the butcher's shop."

"You killed them, Dena? Oh, my God. You killed them?"

"No, not me. Him! It! Something like I've never seen before."

"*Dena, slow down. You aren't making any sense. Who killed those white men?*"

"*A monster,*" Dena said. "*A monster killed them, Adie. Do you remember that man? That man from a long time ago when we were children?*"

"*What man, Dena?*" Adie tried to pretend like she didn't know what her sister was talking about.

"*The man, Adie! The man with the roses!*"

"*She's talking about me, my sweet Adie.*"

Both girls screamed and clutched on to each other. They hadn't even heard anyone sneak up on them. They spun around and saw the man, dressed in a suit and overcoat, standing in the entrance of their small kitchen. Dena's eyes searched his face and his hands, but he was not the monster she last saw. She was confused and didn't understand what was going on, but she held on to Adie like her life depended on it. She was not going to let her sister take a step closer to whatever he was.

"*He's the one who killed those men,*" Dena whispered.

"*You mean the ones who were trying to steal your innocence from you?*" the man said. "*The ones who were going to kill you and stuff you into the trash cans like you were nothing? He*" *was planning on taking your dress and giving it to his wife as if you never existed. Now ask yourself this, Dena: are you sure you are angry at the right person?"*

"But," Dena stuttered, shaking her head from side to side, *"what are you? I saw you change. You aren't a person. You aren't even a man!"*

"Fair enough."

"I remember you," Adie whispered. *"You're the one who gave me the roses that smelled like apple pastries. I've never forgotten you, and how you moved so fast that night. I always knew you couldn't just be a man."* Adie released Dena and went toward him.

"Adie, no!"

"How did you get in here?" Adie pondered.

"The window. It wasn't locked, although it should have been."

"Are you chastising us?" Adie couldn't help the small laugh that escaped her lips. She'd gotten close enough to him to run her fingers down the sides of his face.

"Adie, stop."

"He isn't here to hurt us, Dena. If he were, he would have done it already," Adie said and focused her attention back to him. "He's been following us for years. Isn't that right?"

"I knew I was not as discreet as I had hoped to be." The man flashed her a dazzling smile.

"No, you weren't," Adie said. "I would catch glimpses of you. I even saw you on the boat on our way here to America. I always blamed it on my overactive imagination, but now I know what I saw is true."

"You have always been special, Adie, both of you," he said. "Something has drawn me back to you for years. Your blood is strong."

"What is your name?"

"Dracula is the name that the people have come to know me as. But I have adopted the name Daron."

Both Adie and Dena looked taken aback. They, like everyone else, had heard the stories of the creature that lived off of human blood. The story of Dracula was told to scare children into never wanting to be outside at nighttime. It was told that he was cursed to walk the earth for eternity with no soul and that was what made him so merciless. He envied mortals so much that their blood had become sweet in taste to him. Dena thought it was just a story to keep the children in check, but after what she witnessed she was having seconds thoughts.

"You're a—"

"The only vampire," Daron informed them. "Made by witches. A bat, human blood, and a powerful spell."

"Witches don't exist."

"I'm not supposed to either."

Dena was quiet, and she blinked her eyes a few times. She didn't understand what was going on, or why it was happening. What she did know was that, although she was skeptical, she did not find the monster in her home to be a threat. He did not look at them with eyes that wanted to cause them pain. She couldn't describe what the look in them was, but it was something else. He focused his attention on Dena and only Dena.

"I apologize for even allowing them to touch you," he said. "I only waited for them to pull you into the alley so that I could attack them in the shadows. Trust me, if the town found out I was here, everything would go into flames. I know from experience."

"Why are you here then?"

"To bring you back to my home with me."

"This is our home."

"Is it really?" Daron raised his eyebrow. "Do you want to live forever shunned just because your skin is darker than the superior race? Do you want to forever not feel safe to walk out of your home?"

"No," Dena heard herself whisper.

"Then come with me, and together we will be our own superior race!"

"Come with you, as in become what you are?" she asked.

"Yes."

"A monster?"

"An immortal being. With more power than you could ever imagine."

"Is that why you have been following us?" Adie butted in. "Because you want us to join you forever? Why us?"

"I have been on a search for a very long time for blood that smells as rich as yours. Only the richest of blood can mix with the blood of the most ancient. And in you, I found not one, but two. You will be fast." He demonstrated this by appearing behind them in the blink of an eye, and they had to whip around again. "You will be strong." He demonstrated this by pulling the front door off of its hinges with no effort at all. "And I will bestow upon you gifts that will last you an eternity."

"Gifts?"

"Yes, special powers to children created directly from me. Together, we will create a race unmatched. Together, we will be what the mortals should have been. I, of course, will give the both of you a choice. It is up to you."

"If we say no, will you kill us?" Adie asked.

"No, my sweet girl. I could never dream of hurting the two of you. I, however, cannot lie. I would be very disappointed."

"What do we have to do?"

"Leave all of this behind." He put his hands up and looked around. "I mean, it's not much, yet it is everything to you, right?"

Both girls nodded.

"If you come with me, you will have riches beyond your wildest dreams. All you have to do is drink."

"Drink what?"

"My blood."

"Gross," Adie said and made a face. Dena nudged her, and she made a face. "What? It sounds disgusting. And if he's a million years old, imagine how it tastes."

Daron's smile at that moment was the most genuine one he'd had since his creation. Adie, he knew, would be his favorite. If she agreed to come with him, he knew what gift he would bestow upon her. He let the two women deliberate with each other for a few minutes before they finally turned back to him. It was a decision that should not have been made so hastily but, unbeknownst to them, he was running out of time.

"What say you?" he asked.

"Adie has a question." Dena rolled her eyes.

"First, please get rid of those bodies in the alley—"

"Already done."

"Perfect. And secondly, if we become what you are, will we be young forever?"

"You will look exactly how you do now for eternity."

"Okay," Adie said with a nod. *"We will do it."*

That time when Kesh came back, he wished he didn't have to. It had been so long since he'd seen Adie, and the visions being shown to him by Dena made him feel as though he were right next to her. It was as though Dena was giving him a gift. He hadn't known her before she was a vampire and, while she was the same person, she was so different as a mortal. She was so innocent. Hearing her voice was like music to his ears. It was as sweet as his favorite candy when he too was human.

"Falling in love all over again?" Dena asked studying his face.

"No," Kesh answered. "It is just strange, seeing her that way."

"Those are my most precious memories of my sister," Dena spoke fondly. "She was the best sister anyone could have ever asked for."

"I can tell you were very close. The way she wanted to go fight those men for hurting you was admirable."

"That was Adie for you: fearless, even when she was afraid."

"Was that the only reason she went with Dracula?" Kesh thought about the final question that Adie asked. He wondered if the only reason she had chosen to live a cursed life was to stay young forever. She was a woman he did not peg as being vain, but maybe he had been wrong about her. He didn't have to clarify the question because Dena already knew what he was referring to.

"Don't forget that we were young at the time, Kesh." Dena's eyes sparkled. "Not to mention we're beautiful women. Who wants that to go away? But at the time, if we had known what Dracula would ask us to do after we were turned, I'm not sure if we would have made the same decision. Everything changed so quickly for us. I remember the thirst; it was unbearable. In a matter of a day, my sister and I were turned into monsters."

"Not monsters; vampires," Kesh corrected her.

"Back then we didn't know that there was a difference," she said. "We killed countless numbers of families that first month. That's how long it took to get our hunger under control."

"Dracula did not guide you?"

"He told us we had to find our own way back to the humanity that we had inside of us. That's the same thing he said about our powers. He could not show us where they lay in the deepest parts of ourselves. We had to find them ourselves. We did not yet know it, but he was preparing us for a war. While preparing us, seven more joined us on our path."

"How did Adie find out that she had the gift to reproduce when the other Ancients did not?"

Dena looked away from Kesh. Kesh waited for her lips to part, but they did not. Kesh had a notion that there was yet something else that he did not know about Adie. Dena's brow furrowed and that was the first time since he'd met her that he saw her anything close to angry. Her eyes grew distant, and it seemed like her body was with him, but her mind was not. She remained that way for a while before she finally blinked and found the breath to speak again.

"We trusted him. He was the only thing that made sense to us for so long. He constantly told us how special we were, and how much he loved us. He made us believe in him, but in the end, everything just felt like a big lie. When I found out the true nature of the reason we were created, I did not want this curse anymore. It was too late, of course. The witches created Dracula to fight another one of their creations that had gone bad."

"The Ancient Lykans."

"Yes. He was created specifically to defeat them."

"But he didn't want to fight."

"Exactly. The one thing that the witches didn't count on was that Dracula did not want any part of the war. He created us without their knowledge."

"Why?"

"Because the only ones with enough power to kill Dracula were his creators. If they had known of his treachery, he would have been killed. He used the witches' magic to craft us in his image. He made us damn near invincible. The last thing the witches wanted were more powerful beings to threaten their existence."

"What happened?"

"What happened?" Dena scoffed. "The day of the Great War, he fled, leaving us to fight alongside the witches alone. We didn't even know what was coming. Adie, my poor Adie, was heartbroken."

"What did they do to you? The witches, I mean."

"What could they do? They had no choice but to fight with us. Let me show you."

"Dena!" Adie burst into Dena's chamber with tears running down her face. She was breathing so fast it sounded like she was gasping for air. The sun had just come up, but the dark cloaks over the windows prevented even a lick of sunlight to enter the room.

Dena was in the mirror brushing her hair when her thought process was interrupted. "Adie, what is it you want? I thought we talked about you knocking."

She couldn't hide the irritation that she had with her sister right then. The two of them had been on the outs for some time now, and it was Adie's fault. But when she turned to see Adie's tearstained face, the protective big sister in her came out. She jumped up from the chair of her vanity and held her arms open just in time for Adie to fall into them. Adie sobbed into her shoulder and shook violently.

"What is it, my dear Adie? Tell me. What is it?"

"They're gone," Adie whispered into Dena's neck. "They have fled from the castle."

"Who has fled? Tep and the others?"

"No! Daron and Ajani. He took my son!"

"No!" Dena pushed Adie away from her as gently as she could in her shocked state. She used her speed to see if what Adie was saying had any truth to it. She stopped so suddenly *that the back of her robe whipped in the air. She stood in the doorway of the room Adie shared with Daron and saw that what Adie said was the truth. There was no trace of Daron or the toddler.*

Dena clutched her stomach and dropped to the ground. Ever since Daron had moved them all into his castle, Dena had an aching feeling at the back of her mind that something was not right. Now she was sure. Why had he left so suddenly? Where had he taken her nephew and why?

She felt Adie appear behind her and she struggled back to her feet. "How long has he been gone?"

"I don't know. I woke up and neither one was there. I tried to run outside to find them, but I realized at the last second that my ring was no longer on my finger. I would have burned to a crisp."

Instinctively Dena's eyes shot to her own hand, and she didn't see her ring on the middle finger of her right hand. The rings were crafted by him and allowed them all to walk in the daylight. Daron must have gone in all of their rooms and removed their rings so they would not come searching for him when he fled.

The other vampires turned by Daron found them. Tep, Constance, Lira, Xion, Eron, Brax, and Rain all held alarmed looks on their faces. They harbored the same emotions as Adie and Dena.

"So it's true? He has left us to bear this curse forever alone?"

"Why would he do this?" Dena tried to make sense of everything before she fainted. "I don't understand. Why would he abandon us this way?"

The sound of the double front doors to the castle being forced open grasped all of their attention. The nine of them ran to the staircase banister and looked three stories down to see if it was Daron. It wasn't. They were met with faces they'd never seen before. There were five women, dressed in elegant black gowns. Their faces were beautiful, but so hideous at the same time, unlike anything the nine vampires had ever seen.

"He abandoned you because he knew we were coming." The one who spoke was front and center. The matted braids in her hair hung loosely on her shoulders as she addressed the nine. Her teeth were black, and her voice seemed to echo throughout the entire castle.

"Witches," Tep whispered and leapt down to face them fearlessly. "Why have you come to our castle? What is it you want?"

"Your castle?" The witch in the front cackled. "You mean my castle!"

Her voice boomed, and she raised her arms in the air. Every piece of furniture and every portrait hanging on the walls shook. She was not to be trifled with, and she wanted to make that clear. She blinked, and her dark eyes changed to a bright emerald green.

"I am Aika, high priestess of the Illuminated coven. Leader of all witches. Your creator has left you because you all have been created unlawfully with the magic of witches. It is a crime to be punished by death!"

She flicked her wrist, and Tep began to choke on thin air. It felt as if a hand had a grasp on his heart and was squeezing the life out of him. Right when he was about to take his last breath, something moved as fast as lightning and sent Aika crashing into the wall. The impact put a big hole in the wall, and she fell to the ground. Her hold on Tep released and he was able to see his savior.

Dena breathed heavily and placed her foot back on the ground. "I will not let you kill my brother for the crime of another," Dena's voice boomed as she placed back on the ground the foot that had sent Aika flying. "I don't care who you are, or what coven you are from, witch. Leave here now while you live."

Aika quickly regained her footing and glared at Dena. She took a step toward her, but as soon as she did, the other seven surrounded the two in front of her. She didn't know if she was angry or curious; maybe it was a little of both. She flicked her wrist once more and sent the vampires surrounding Dena to the sides. Dena tried to move her own feet but found that she was frozen in place. Aika didn't stop walking until she and Dena were nose to nose. She took one finger and traced the side of Dena's face with an eerie smile.

"Dena," she said. "I like that. Do you know why Dracula . . . Excuse me. I think he goes by Daron now. Do you know why he created you nine?"

"Because he wanted companionship," Dena answered, and all five of the witches cackled loudly.

"No, my dear child. Daron is a selfish creature. He did a good job making you believe that he loved you. No, no, no. Daron only loves himself. You see, I created him. I made him to protect us, but he's nowhere to be found when we need his protecting. So, don't you see? He made you to do his job for him."

"Protecting? Protect you from what?"

"From them!" Aika placed both palms on the sides of Dena's face and telepathically showed her the horrors known as the Ancient Lykans. Dena gasped as she watched the huge beasts destroy entire civilizations. They were powerful, more powerful than anything she'd ever seen and, for the first time in a long time, she felt fear.

"Those monsters are known to the humans as werewolves," Aika whispered in her ear. "They are more ferocious than even you. Their hunger outweighs your thirst by the thousands, because, you see, they never get full. They are always hungry. And now they want to kill everything, including us witches."

"And Daron was supposed to defeat them for you?"

"Yes," Aika told her. "We built this castle for his solitude and promised to never bother him until we needed him to fight the Great War. He felt our presence coming, and he knew what that meant."

"So he fled." Dena closed her eyes suddenly understanding. "He fled like a coward and left us to fight his fight."

"No, my dear child," Aika said releasing her hold on all of them. "He left you all to die." Her eyes found Adie's and she saw the sadness in them. She searched Adie's mind and felt a grief that was even hard for her to bear. "Oh, my Adie. You fell in love with him and even bore his child. I can feel the anger consuming you as you stand there looking at me."

Aika stepped back making "tsk tsk" sounds with her tongue. The green was gone from her eyes, and she pondered over her decision. They didn't have much time. She knew immediately after the portal opened that Daron was no longer in the castle. But, still, she felt such power residing in the walls. She never would have expected to find nine when she only created one.

"How did Daron create you?"

"We drank from his blood."

"And the powers?"

Dena looked taken aback by the question before she remembered that Aika had read her mind to figure out her name.

"I didn't have to read your mind to know you have them. I can feel them. How did he bestow these gifts?"

"As we drank from him, he recited words. I don't remember quite what he said, but I think it was a spell."

"That damned Daron." Aika shook her head. "Show me."

Dena hesitated at first, but Aika's eyes flashed green again, and she decided to do what she was asked. She concentrated her mind and, although she felt them fight against her, she was still able to lift the four witches behind Aika off their feet. Aika's eyes widened with surprise because she could tell the witches were fighting against Dena.

"Interesting," Aika murmured. "Release them."

Dena did as she was told again and the witches looked as if somebody had ruffled their feathers greatly. When one of them got her wits about her, she cleared her throat. Her hair was barely an inch from her head, and her nose was pointed in a downward angle. She was plumper than the other four, but the look in her eyes was just as deadly.

"What are we to do with them, High Priestess? Are we to dispose of them?"

"You know we cannot do that, Tabitha. Not with the Lykans on our heels. Daron bestowed upon them the gifts of illusion, telekinesis, fire, ice, clairvoyance, energy snatching, precognition, shapeshifting, and life. They are powerful. They will fight for us."

"Why would I fight for you when you just tried to kill me?" Tep spat.

"Because you have no choice." Aika narrowed her eyes at him. *"Daron took your rings with him, did he not?"*

"Yes," Adie answered.

"Then that means you cannot leave this castle for another eight hours. The Lykans will be here in five."

She shared with the rest of them the same vision that she shared with Dena, and looks of terror spread across their faces. Lira's hand latched on to Constance's, and they both looked to Dena.

"We are supposed to fight them?" Eron demanded to know. *"Those things look like they have been in many battles. We have never been in one."*

"The only fights we have been in are fights with the humans. We know nothing about this war that you bring to our doorstep!" Tep shouted. *"We will all perish."*

The entire room erupted into a fit of arguments. Aika felt as though she were arguing with a group of small children. They went back and forth, wasting valuable time for what seemed like forever, with no outcome.

A meek voice then spoke. It was as small as a mouse, but the entire room quieted to hear the skinny witch with the long gray hair. It was *like her voice alone was a spell, and Aika spun around the second she heard it. "If there was one thing Daron was right about in this whole situation, it is that you all have the richest blood. When Aika created Dracula—Daron, as you know him—she created him so that his blood would kill anyone who dared to bite him or drink it. You nine were able to drink it and transform. If Aika won't say it, I will say it for the coven: we need you."*

"Mila," Aika whispered, "you haven't spoken a word in a century."

"Because there has not been a graver time than now for my voice to be heard," Mila said and turned her attention back to the nine. "Fight with us and help us rid the world of this great evil we have created."

"What do we get?" Lira couldn't resist asking.

"Will you help me find my son?" Adie's voice said right after.

"We will give you everything you need: new rings, a new fortress that no one can find, and we will search high and low for your child, Adie. You have our word."

"And why should the word of a witch mean anything to us?" Dena asked.

Aika looked fondly at Dena, and Dena was taken aback. She was wondering if it was her the witch was seeing. But when she heard Aika's voice but did not see her lips move, she understood.

"You are strong, almost as strong as your creator." *Aika's voice echoed in Dena's head.* "They look up to you whether you know it or not."

How do you know that? Dena thought.

"I have seen their minds. You will be their leader, and they will follow you into a black pit of doom if you lead them there. In one thousand years, no one has ever been able to lay a hand on me, and you did it so easily. For that, I owe you allegiance. Fight with us. We don't have much time."

Why should I trust you when Daron did not?

"Why would you base your own decision off of the morals of a creature that left your sister with a broken heart?"

Her question lingered in Dena's head and echoed what seemed like thousands of times before Dena finally pursed her full lips. She didn't know what to say, and when she glanced back at the others, they had confusion in their eyes. It was obvious that they were wondering what kind of exchange was going on between the two women. When Dena turned back to Aika, the fond glow was gone from the witch's eyes, only to be replaced with sadness.

What makes you sad? *Dena asked.*

"You." *Aika's thought came with so much sorrow that Dena's eyes began to water.* "You remind me so much of my daughter."

What happened to her?

"Murdered, in cold blood."

She then shared with Dena the memory of watching her only child get her heart ripped out by the Ancient Lykan named Mezza. Every emotion that Aika felt at the time of the massacre was passed to Dena, who began to sob. Aika's daughter was not the only one slaughtered that night.

"They killed your entire coven," *Dena breathed out loud.* "You five are all there are left, aren't you? And they know you're here."

"Yes. Mezza found the location to this castle in one of our spell books. The one with the incantation on how to open the portal."

"Okay."

"Okay?"

"Yes. We will fight with you."

"Dena!"

"What?"

"We will die!"

"We will fight for what is right!" *Dena whipped around to face them.* "If we do not fight today, then we will have to fight tomorrow. Or the

next day. Don't you see? Those things want this
world for themselves! Do you think that they
will stop with the witches? No! So let's do what
we were created to do!"

Dena turned to Adie. "Sister, I am so sorry
for your loss. I can't imagine how you feel. But
these beasts are coming our way. I need you
to pull together all of your strength and use all
of your anger to fight beside me. Once we are
done, I will stop at nothing to find my nephew.
Okay?"

Adie stepped forward and blinked away the
tears in her eyes. She nodded and moved a curl
of hair from her eyes. "Okay, sister. I will follow
you into battle as long as these witches keep
their word."

Slowly but surely the other vampires agreed
to fight as well. Aika took one of Adie's hands
in hers, and Dena's in the other. Her eyes were
on the other vampires, silently telling them to
grab a hand too. When they did, they formed
a circle, and the four witches on the outskirts
began mumbling words that sounded meshed
together.

"What are you doing?" Dena asked.

"Making your minds one. I am giving you all
the power to read minds and feelings, along
with sharing them with others. This will be
important if you hope to defeat the Lykans."

Kesh watched the Great War flash before his eyes. It was a wonder that all nine survived it. The Ancient Lykans were malicious, more so than he could have ever dreamed. He did not know if either of the clans were going to be ready and up to fight that.

"They will be, as long as you lead them," Dena told him. "Never forget who you are, Kesh."

"How can I forget who I am when I don't even know who I am?"

"You don't?"

"I mean, now I do, but up until this point, everything has been false. Adie—"

"Yes, she had a child with Daron. She fell in love with him the moment he turned her. There was no bringing her back from that. When she bore his child, she thought nothing could be sweeter, but of course, she didn't know of her lover's sinister plan for her."

"Did you ever locate her son?"

"No," Dena said sadly. "No one has seen him or Daron since long ago. That was another reason Adie left. She felt like we hadn't held up our end of the bargain. And I tried to, I really did. But a hundred years passed, and then another—"

"But still no sign of them."

"No," she said. "And sometimes I wonder to myself if I checked the right places."

"There's no telling if they are even still alive?"

"Ajani, no. There is no telling. But Daron, oh, he's still alive. I can feel him. And when I see him, I'm going to kill him. He has given me eternal life, but with that came eternal pain. This is no way to live. Before I met Adirah and baby Adis, I was torn apart. I have been torn for so long, but they put me back together. As they have done to you."

"Did Adie . . ."

"Did she really love you?" Dena asked him and placed a warm palm on his cheek. "Oh, I believe she cared for you deeply and even wanted to love you as much. But my sister had a hole so big in her heart, I honestly think it was better that she didn't. But Adirah loves you, with every fiber of her being. I can feel it. And that is what you should hold on to. Go find her. Make it right."

"I can't." Kesh shook his head once. "Not right now. I deserve her anger because I do not deserve her love. I think it would be better for me to go to the Malum camp alone. I don't want the fact that we are not getting along to be the reason to throw us off our game. Talum and Calum's love for each other is the only thing that saved them last time. I don't want our dislike to be the reason for our doom."

"Understood. When will you leave?"

"Tonight. Please tell Adirah that I am sorry."

"Why don't you tell her yourself when you come back?"

With that, Dena disappeared. Kesh knew that she didn't teleport, but her speed was something never seen by vampires or humans.

"If I come back," he muttered.

Adirah stirred in her sleep. Something wasn't right. Although she was still angry with Kesh, she did not want to go to sleep that night without him by her side. When she fell asleep, he was there, and baby Adis was in his crib not too far away from the bed. However, when she opened her eyes in the middle of the night, the baby was still where she'd left him, but Kesh was no longer in the bed with her.

She sat up and ran to the hallway. Looking both ways down each long hallway, she fell backward on one of the walls and held her hand to her chest.

"Don't you dare let a tear drop."

Adirah blinked her eyes, and through her blurry vision she could make out Lira standing there. She had appeared out of thin air, it seemed, but Adirah was grateful for her presence.

"He left me," she whispered.

"Not because he wanted to," Lira told her. "I overheard him speaking with Dena. He didn't think you'd forgive him in time to face the Malum, so he decided to go alone."

"No!"

"Yes," Lira said and shrugged her arms. "But good for you he literally just left. He and Dena are on their way to the passageway now. If you get dressed, you might be able to catch him. The passage only stays open for fifteen seconds after one of us touches it."

Adirah didn't need to be told twice. When she was dressed in her most comfortable slacks, boots, shirt, and leather jacket, she leaned over Adis's crib. "Will you look after him?"

"Yes." Lira's voice was directly behind her. "With my life."

"Okay," Adirah said and kissed her son lovingly on his forehead. "I need you to do something for me."

"What's that?"

"Lend me your speed."

Adirah held her hand out, and Lira looked at it, smiling mischievously. "Only if you're sure. Breathe!"

On Lira's last word, she grabbed Adirah's arm. Adirah suddenly felt like she was on a ride that she wanted badly to get off of. The sights around her weren't a blur; they simply didn't exist. When they stopped moving, they weren't in the castle anymore, nowhere near it for that matter. By the time Adirah took her next breath, she was in front of Kesh and Dena. Dena's palm had just gone up to open the passage, but she stopped when she saw Lira and Adirah.

"I knew I felt someone eavesdropping on my conversation earlier."

"Sorry." Lira shrugged with a sheepish smile. "Adie wasn't the only sucker for love."

Adirah walked up to Kesh and pushed his chest. "You were going to leave me? Seriously!"

"Adirah."

"Don't Adirah me! You were just going to go! And what? Fight both Talum and Calum by yourself?"

"If I had to, yes."

"Do you know how stupid that is? What are you trying to do, make it so you don't come home to Adis and me?"

"Dira," Kesh tried again, "you were so upset earlier, the look on your face tore me apart inside. I didn't want to risk your heart anymore by taking you on this journey with me. But, before I go, I just want you to know that I love you. Not because you are kin to someone else I loved centuries ago, but because you are Adirah

Messa. You fill me up in places that I didn't even know existed. I learned to live without Adie, but I cannot learn to live without you. I just wouldn't be able to. I'd stake myself right in the heart."

Adirah not only heard the sincerity in his tone, she saw it in his eyes. While the news that he was once in love with Adie was still unsettling, there was nothing that she could do about it. It was the past, and the past was that for a reason. She couldn't deny her heart's affection for him, nor did she want to. Her feet had a mind of their own when they led her into his arms. They embraced while the two Ancients looked at them, both with small smiles on their faces.

"I expect more than just you two when you return," Dena said and closed her eyes as if she were summoning something inside herself. She placed her hand forward, seemingly touching nothing but air. Soon the entire scene in front of them began to ripple like it had before and they could see through to the other side. "Good luck to you both. There is a car waiting for you on the other side."

Hand in hand, Adirah and Kesh stepped through the passageway. Sure enough, on the other side, parked in the snow by the mountain, was the same SUV they drove to get there.

"Dammit," Adirah mumbled. "I was hoping for a BMW this time."

Kesh grinned at her as they trekked through the snow. As he helped her in the SUV, he told himself that if they all survived what was coming, he would make her his wife.

Chapter 13

Tiev drove his car to the gated entrance of the Malum camp and waited for the gate to be opened. He wore sunglasses at the tip of his nose, and one arm was hanging out of his Mercedes coupe. One of the Malum gate watchers approached the car slowly. Although they'd seen the car several times before, they always gave him a hard time.

"Sefu." The male vampire said the word as if it tasted like mud. He was tall and looked strong, but Tiev knew he would tear him in half in a duel. The malice in his voice was to be expected; they were enemies, after all.

"Malum." Tiev smirked. "Will you please tell your king I am here? I do not like waiting."

"I don't care what you don't like! You not only are a scum to us, you are a traitor to your own people."

"Botsu!"

The other watching the gate came and put his hand on Botsu's arm to calm him down. While he did not say anything else, Botsu snatched away and gave Tiev a glare that he could not forget.

"Thanks, Botsu." Tiev waved him away. "Now, like I said, open the gate."

Tiev wasn't going to let a couple of nobody vampires ruin his mood. He was there on business, and it didn't matter if anyone there liked him. Soon his name would demand the respect of all vampires alike if he played his hand right.

He drove his car up to the round driveway of the house and, as always, he admired the home. He said that, once he could get all of the Sefu to follow him and only him, he would move them all into a bigger estate. At the moment, they were all so comfortable where they were. Some, it seemed, had grown accustomed to the college life. He was sure some of them really thought that they were students and the same age as the humans around them. He hoped that the knowledge that soon they'd have to move anyway would be enough to sway them more toward his favor, especially with Kesh being gone in the wind.

Parking his car, he stepped out and headed toward the front door. He didn't even get the chance to knock before it flew open and Calum greeted him. She was wearing a black dress with thin straps that hugged her curvy brown body. There was a slit at the side of her right leg that came up to her thigh. Tiev couldn't help the fact that his eyes traveled her body like a plane trying to get to its destination.

"Calum, looking as lovely as ever." He offered her a fake smile.

She stared at him, most likely trying to read his thoughts. He'd mastered keeping himself undetectable, as any vampire should in his position, and he was pleased at the look of irritation that crossed her face.

"Tiev, I wish I could say the same about you." She stepped back and let him in. "Talum is just out back."

She led him through the spacious home to the kitchen in the back of the house. It was large with yellow walls and a tiled floor. There was an island in the center of the kitchen with a deep sink in the middle of it. The décor was simply elegant. Whoever had designed the whole house deserved a medal.

"It's a shame that you can't enjoy your meals in here," Tiev said looking around. "What a waste."

They walked around the tall island and made their way to the glass patio door that would take them to the backyard. Through the glass, he was able to make out Talum standing with his back to them. The only thing that Tiev could see was that Talum was holding a glass and taking sips from it. When Calum and Tiev presented themselves to him, he turned to face them.

"I see you have learned the skill of cloaking your thoughts, Tiev," Talum said in an impressed tone. "If I weren't expecting you, I wouldn't have even sensed you coming. Scotch?"

"Thank you," Tiev said after Talum poured the glass and handed it to him. "I always took you for a bourbon type of man."

"I dabble a bit in both," Talum replied and took another sip of his Scotch. He sucked his teeth and made an "ahhh" sound. "I take it you come bringing me news of the Sefu clan."

"Yes," Tiev stated. "Partially. Kesh has not been seen or heard from in over a year. It is safe to say that he has abandoned his clan."

"And?"

"And? Don't you see? This is the perfect time to strike!"

Talum paced on the concrete deck, swirling his drink around. Calum had taken a seat at the round table protected by the shade given by the wide umbrella. She stared intently at the two of them, interested in what her king would say.

"Strike as in attack?" Talum asked.

"Yes."

"Funny. I was under the impression that you wanted to become their king. But I could be wrong."

"No. You are right, but there is a process to everything." Tiev gave a slick smile. "You see, we can give the illusion of an attack. A few casualties, of course, and then—"

"You come in to save the day," Calum interrupted.

"Exactly! They will have no choice but to name me as their king and then you and I can both go our separate ways. We make a peace treaty, and our clans will never have to cross paths again. Nothing of this meeting can ever happen. We would seal it with a blood oath, of course."

Talum let Tiev's words play in his ears over and over. At first, he was going to tell Tiev no and send him on his way. But the more he thought about it, the more he seemed to like the idea. "Under one condition."

"Whatever you want."

"When Kesh does resurface, he will not have the protection of the Sefu clan. You will let me kill him."

"Done," Tiev said with no hesitation.

Talum nodded. "I will retrieve the paper we will seal the blood oath on."

When he left Tiev was left with Calum. They did not speak to each other, but Tiev did sit down at the table with her. It took everything in him to hold back the smile that threatened to spread across his face.

What a fool. Does he really think that I'm going to let him be the one to finish Kesh off? No. When the Malum attack the Sefu I will be ready and waiting to kill him and his queen. And when Kesh shows his face, I will be ready to kill him too.

He felt someone staring at him, and when he looked to Calum, sure enough, her eyes were on him. She was once again studying him, trying to find her way into his mind. She didn't trust him, he could tell. But she wasn't his problem. Anything that her king told her to do she would do with no questions asked.

"Are you in pain?" she asked.

"No, not at all."

"Then why does your face look like you just got your dick bitten in half?"

In the estate, Talum was upstairs in the bedroom he and Calum shared. That was where he kept his book of laws and agreements. There was something about Tiev that he did not like, but if the vampire tried to go back on the oath, he would have his throat ripped out. Talum's thirst to see Kesh keeled over dead was clouding his judgment when it came to doing business with a clear blood traitor.

Behind him, the door slammed shut, startling him because he did not hear anyone come in after him. "He *is* a blood traitor. Anything to see me dead, though, I presume."

Talum whipped around and was stunned to see Kesh standing very much alive in front of him. In his estate! "Kesh! How?"

"How did I read your thoughts? It seems like you only had your thoughts cloaked when you were outside with Tiev and Calum."

"No; how did you get in here?" Talum instantly crouched into a battle position.

"Put your claws away, brother," Kesh said and made to take a step toward Talum.

That step turned into many, as Kesh used his speed to get directly in front of Talum. The element of surprise was on his side because Talum's mouth was wide open the way Kesh needed it to be. He took the elixir from his pocket and squeezed a drop on Talum's tongue. When Talum tried to attack, Kesh put his hand out.

"Stop!"

Kesh's command didn't fall on deaf ears. Talum stopped in the middle of his motion. The only things that he had control over were his eyes. It was like his entire body had been taken control of. Kesh was the master, and Talum was his dummy.

"Sit and relax."

Talum, once again, did as he was told. He just knew it was the end for him. Why else would Kesh go through the trouble of sneaking into his camp? It had all been so easy. All that preparation, all of the training, was for nothing. Kesh still won.

From the desk chair Talum was in, he watched Kesh's movements. He wondered how Kesh would kill him. Would he rip his heart from his chest so that Talum could watch the stake go through it? Or maybe he would strip him of the ring on his finger so that the sun could turn him to dust.

"Surprisingly, I am not going to do any of those things." Kesh's voice was low and deep. "If this were a year ago, you would already be dead; but now we have bigger problems on our hands. Problems even bigger than the ones between you and me."

What problems are bigger than the ones between our two clans?

"Problems that you may think are a myth. Problems that threaten every vampire life on this earth. You are strong, Talum. I know you can sense it coming too, just like I can. You haven't been able to sleep a full night, have you? Or shake the feeling that something is close?"

Kesh saw glimpses of Talum's thoughts flashing in his own head. They stopped on a recent memory of both Talum and Calum in the library of the estate. Kesh saw the passage that Talum had read. "The prophecy."

Prophecy? Then it is true: your son is the golden child.

"Yes."

And that means the Ancient Lykans . . .

"One or both of them have awakened. With the full moon approaching, the Lykans will be at full power to attack."

Attack who?

"The Ancient vampires."

They are a myth!

At that moment Kesh used his powers to share his recent memories with Talum. He didn't show him their location, but Kesh showed him that they were very much alive.

"They need us. They cannot fight the Lykans alone and expect to win. They will perish trying. You can't make that oath with Tiev. He is not to be trusted. We must unite the Sefu and the Malum as one if we expect to win. We have the most powerful vampire clans in strength and numbers. We cannot let the Lykans win this war."

If it had not been for you and your queen, none of us would be in this situation. You are the ones who bore the child who woke the monsters up! Why should I fight to protect it?

"This war was inevitable. It was going to come whether we liked it or not." Kesh's voice was a low growl. He did not like the way that Talum spoke about his son, but he also remembered his promise to Dena. "I created you, Talum, not because you were weak prey but because you were strong. We were once brothers: brothers who had the same vision for our people. I never wanted it to be this way. There should not be two clans; there should only be one."

One that only you rule over, right?

"Do you think I wanted this? This was never something I asked for. I never had a choice like you to become a king, Talum. When I was born again, this is who I was. I was created by an Ancient, and that makes me the king of all vampires."

An Ancient? That explained why he was stronger and faster than the rest of them. It also explained why he was able to survive so long without feeding the last time they battled. It was right then that it dawned on Talum that, no matter what he did, Kesh would always be the alpha of the two of them. Not by choice, but by blood. Talum's thirst for power had held him for centuries and caused him to lose someone he truly felt was his brother. All because he felt that he would never be Kesh's equal if he wasn't a king too.

"Just because I am king does not mean I do not view you as my equal. You are strong, Talum, and a fierce warrior. We won't win this war if you are not by my side. I refuse to fight it if you are not there."

What am I supposed to do?

"You must call a meeting with all of the Malum, and explain to them what is happening. I do not wish to be here in secret, and they will not fight with me if they hate me. They will not stand for me if they do not trust me."

Why should I trust you?

"Because I am prepared to fight not only for my son, but for all vampires alike. Including you."

When Talum walked back outside, Tiev and Calum were still where he'd left them. They were both sitting in an awkward silence until he presented himself.

"I was starting to think you ran off on me," Tiev joked.

"And leave you with my queen?" Talum raised his eyebrow at him as if he'd said the most absurd thing. "Never."

Tiev gave an impatient smile and glanced at Talum's hands in search of the papers he was supposed to get. When he didn't see them there, he checked the pockets of his jeans. Still nothing. "You don't have the papers."

"Ah." Talum put his finger in the air as if he was suddenly remembering something that he'd forgotten. "About that."

"What do you mean, about that? I thought we had a deal! I said you could kill Kesh if we make this deal."

"Come on, Tiev." Talum cocked his head at the vampire. "You and I both know that you wanted that pleasure all to yourself. Plus—"

"Plus, you would never be a true king to the Sefu."

The voice made both Calum and Tiev jump in their seats. Tiev jumped up and faced Kesh with his fangs out. Calum jumped on top of the table and hissed violently when both Kesh and Adirah stepped down on the concrete deck, looking like they owned the place.

"Adirah!"

"Calum!"

Adirah felt her nails grow along with her fangs. There was nothing that she'd rather do than rip her teeth out one by one, but Kesh's hand on her shoulder stopped her from attacking.

"What's going on here, Talum?" Tiev growled. "Why is he here? And why have you not yet killed him?"

"Because I didn't want to," Talum said. "It dawned on me while I was upstairs that a blood traitor like you would never keep his word. Our agreement is off."

"And as the king of vampires, I banish you, blood traitor." Kesh's lip curled as he spoke to Tiev. "There was one point when I would trust you with my life. But now, here you are, bartering with it. What changed?"

"Everything between us changed when you killed Vila," Tiev said. "You did not even give her a chance to explain herself. You just killed her."

"She, like you, tried to kill me. That is treason. I did not want to kill Vila, but she forced my hand."

"She forced your hand because you put a mortal above your own clan."

"Adirah is a vampire, just like you and me."

"She is now," Tiev sneered at her.

The hairs on the back of Kesh's neck stood up, and he felt himself preparing for an attack. But the attack never came. Tiev must have realized that he was outnumbered, and he backed up slowly before running around the house to the front. Talum made to go after him, but Kesh stopped him.

"Let him flee. I will deal with him when I go speak to my people."

Although Kesh had given Talum control back over his own body, Talum still did what he was asked. Calum, still perched on the table, looked back and forth from Talum to Kesh.

"What's going on, Talum? And why are you listening to his commands?"

"We are uniting the clans," he answered simply.

"Uniting what!"

"I will explain later when I address the entire court."

"No, Talum, you will explain now."

Talum looked at Calum and could tell just by the upset look on her face that she was not going to let him drop it without telling her exactly what happened. He sighed and quickly briefed her on everything that was going on.

"We can't risk continuing this feud with each other when a far greater danger is heading right toward us. It will feed on our division and rip us completely apart."

"So we must unite," Kesh said.

"Under one condition." Talum looked at Kesh.

"What condition?" Calum and Adirah asked in unison.

"The two of you battle," Talum said looking Calum squarely in the eye. "You have not been training for nothing, my love."

"And you have so much anger built up inside of you, Dira," Kesh said.

"We have the perfect training area for you to let it all out. Calum, lead the way."

"You mean, you won't be there to watch?"

"Kesh and I have much to discuss, so I apologize. I will not be there to witness this fight."

"Kesh . . ."

But Kesh was already back inside of the house, and Talum quickly followed. He shut the patio door behind him and locked it, leaving their women outside.

"What if they kill each other?" Talum asked.

"They won't," Kesh said as he walked. "They must learn how to fight alongside each other. What better way than to have them fight each other?"

Chapter 14

A year had been a long time to wait, but there they were, standing in the clearing facing off with each other. Both Adirah and Calum were changed into their vampire forms, breathing heavily. Both women were thirsty for victory, but only one would come out on top.

"I have waited a long time to be able to taste your blood," Calum hissed with a low laugh. "How unexpected that you would walk right into my home."

"It wasn't hard," Adirah spat back. "Knocking the two vampires out at the front gate was effort-less. Just like I'm sure defeating you is going to be. I did it before. We drove all day and night just so I could do it again!"

On the last word, the two women ran full speed at each other, colliding with each other at the last second. Adirah was sure that her first strike would knock Calum on her back, but she stood her ground. The two women fought like

ferocious beasts. Each attack they made was
relentless as they were both hoping it was the
attack that would be their last. Calum ate one of
Adirah's punches and threw one back her way,
catching her in the jaw. Adirah flew backward at
the power of Calum's punch, but she landed on
her feet, skidding. She pressed her hand to the
ground and used her claws to slow her down.

"Ahhh!" Calum had run and taken a great leap
in the air in hopes of hitting Adirah's face into
the ground. Adirah dodged the attack at the last
second and countered by chopping Calum hard
in her throat. She then followed through with
a quick left jab and a kick to the stomach that
sent Calum flying through the air again. Using
her speed, Adirah ran in the same direction and,
instead of landing, Calum was met with a hard
fist that sent her plummeting to the ground. The
power of Adirah's attack caused the ground to
dent under Calum's body.

Although in pain, Calum was not ready to give
up. The mistake Adirah made was thinking that
she'd already won. As soon as her guard was
down, Calum attacked again. She jumped back
up and grabbed Adirah by the neck, slamming
her to the ground. She put all her power into her
fists and pounded repeatedly into Adirah's chest
until blood spat from her mouth. Adirah was

defenseless as Calum leered over her, watching her prey. That time, she had the advantage.

"I win, Adirah." She smirked and gave a loud battle cry before she raised her claw high and brought it down forcefully.

Adirah clenched her eyes shut and tried to prepare for the pain to come. When it never did, she opened her eyes to peek. Calum's face was inches away from hers, and she was panting. Adirah looked over to Calum's hand that was supposed to be attacking her, and she saw that it was wrist deep into the ground.

"I win even if I don't kill you," Calum said, her voice barely louder than a whisper.

"You might as well just kill me," Adirah said weakly, "if you won."

Calum shook her head. "They would have never left us alone if they really believed we would kill each other." Calum removed her hand from the soil.

Her ears twitched, and she looked to the forest to the right of her. Using her speed, she was gone from in front of Adirah one moment, but back the next. When she returned, she had a rabbit in her hands.

"Here," she said handing Adirah the animal. "Drink. It will help you heal faster."

Adirah didn't think twice about taking the rabbit. She sat up weakly and bit down on the rabbit's neck. It fought violently for a split second but stopped as Adirah sucked the life from it. When she was done, she threw it to the side and wiped what blood she could from her mouth. The pain in her chest was no longer there, and she was able to stand without wincing. They both changed back into their human forms. Neither knew what to say to each other at first, so they just glared into the other's eyes.

"I guess you got what you wanted. A victory." Adirah's words came out hard, but it was only because she was bitter. How did Calum beat her when she had beat her so easily before?

"You fight well for a vampire who does not train for battle."

"How would you know if I train or not?"

"A vampire who is war ready would never quit the fight before it was over. You got me good and expected me to be down for the count. On real war fields, Lykans are ready to fight until their last breath; it does not matter how bruised up they are. That goes for vampires too. Never give up unless there is no possible way that you can move."

"You're giving me battle advice?"

"Maybe," Calum said and nodded back toward the estate. "Come on, before they come looking for us. I wonder how the rest of the Malum took to seeing your man here."

"Probably the same as you. They probably jumped on the nearest table with their fangs out."

She didn't mean to, she really didn't, but Calum felt the laugh come up through the deepest part of her belly and out of her mouth. She got a brief visual of the entire Malum clan doing what she had done, and she thought it was the funniest thing.

"She has a sense of humor?" Adirah pretended to be shocked and put a hand to her chest.

Calum instantly stopped laughing, and the hard expression was back on her face in seconds. She cleared her throat as they walked, but it was too late. She'd already shown Adirah a side of her that rarely got brought out unless she was with Talum. "Sometimes."

"Huh?" Adirah asked.

"Sometimes I smile genuinely. Sometimes I laugh."

"Why only sometimes?"

"I've been around a long time. I've seen a lot of things, done a lot of things that have taken the laughter out of my cold heart. This life will take a toll on you after a while. The only thing that made sense for so long was our feud with the Sefu. But now I'm thinking we . . . I used it to cloak my need for something more. I took my frustration over not feeling complete out on this petty-ass war between—"

"Your brothers and sisters," Adirah said.

"All behind Talum's hunger for power. That was a long time ago, though. Recently I have noticed a shift in him, before you showed up at all. I think he realized his mistake a while ago; it has just taken him until now to realize it. I know he grows tired of seeing vampires kill other vampires. Not only that, I feel like he blames himself for pitting them against each other."

She thought about the Talum she'd first met and the Talum he was at that very moment. The craziest thing was that, throughout all of his changes, it was like she changed with him. When he wore hatred like a sheet of armor, so did she, fighting anyone and everyone who opposed them in any way. Now, Talum showed remorse and compassion. His hatred for Kesh was what started him on his journey in the first place. But after that last battle took place, Calum noticed that only she was training for the next fight. Talum was always somewhere else getting lost in his thoughts. Slowly but surely his hate for Kesh had gone away; she felt it. And since that hatred was gone, there was nothing else to fuel the fire of the feud.

As they walked, she was so lost in her own mind that she almost didn't hear Adirah's soft voice begin to speak. "There is a place, where the Ancients live, where all the vampires live in peace. You know the craziest thing?"

"What?"

"They all have the choice to leave, and come back to this world, but they don't unless they have to. They would rather live in peace."

"How do they feed?"

"They own a blood bank," Adirah answered, remembering something that Constance told her.

"They don't hunt humans?"

"No," Adirah said. "Those ways are long behind them."

"Will we meet them?" Calum's question came out hesitant, and she failed to mask the plea in her voice.

"Yes," Adirah answered. "They want you all to come back with us. If the Malum and the Sefu cooperate, that is."

"They will."

"How do you know?"

"Because our two men are the fiercest leaders ever to grace this earth. If they were powerful separate, imagine what they can do together. No one will want to oppose that. You see how Tiev fled."

By that time the two of them had reached the estate. There was not a vampire in sight but the two at the gate. Calum assumed that they were all inside. There were no loud uproars coming from inside of the estate.

"Maybe they have all agreed to end the divide," Adirah said hopefully.

"Or maybe they have all died from the shock," Calum said. "Either way, let's get in there and see what the hell is going on."

With their differences not too far behind them, the twosome made their way up to the front doors in hopes of walking in on a truce. They both held their breath as they opened the doors to the mansion. Calum raised her eyebrows when she noticed everyone bustling around doing their normal duties. Calum grabbed one of the women walking by her by the arm.

"Where is Talum?"

"I think he's still in the library talking to Kesh." She said it with such ease, like nothing was wrong with her statement at all. She turned her afro head to Adirah and offered a kind smile. "Hello, Adirah. Welcome to our home. I'm sorry that a truce couldn't have been called at a better time, but I am pleased to know that the feud between our clans is over."

Calum released her arm and looked over at Adirah in awe. "What the hell happened while we were gone, Liza?"

"Talum made all of us go into the library."

"And then what happened?"

"He told us that there would be some changes to our lives, and then he brought out Kesh."

"No one opposed?"

"Of course they did." Liza looked at Calum as if she had something on her face. "But given that everyone knows about the birth of their son, and most of us know what the prophecy says, we shut up to listen. And . . ."

"And what?"

"I've been feeling it too."

"Feeling what?"

"It," she said. "It's coming, and I've been feeling it for days now. A few of the others did too. We all spoke up for Kesh. The others knew we wouldn't lie."

"Thank you." Adirah gave her the gratitude she deserved.

"So, is it true?"

"Is what true?"

"Are we really going to go stay with the Ancients?"

"Yes," Adirah said and offered a kind smile. *As soon as we get the Sefu to agree to the truce as well.*

"Then I am ready to go to war." Liza walked off with a big smile on her face after her last statement.

As soon as Liza was gone, Calum ran off in a direction so fast that Adirah had to hurry after her to keep up. When they finally stopped, they were in a library facing both Talum and Kesh. Adirah had a big smile on her face while Calum looked at Talum with wonder on hers.

"So, who won?" Kesh asked casually.

Adirah opened her mouth to answer truthfully, but Calum beat her to the punch. "That does not matter anymore," she said. "We both had our weak moments. If you would like, while you two are here I can begin to train Adirah."

Both Kesh and Talum stood speechless.

"It's inevitable, right? The war is coming. She needs to be ready. Lykans fight like no other beast that I've ever met."

"If it is okay with Kesh, then it is okay with me."

Kesh nodded, giving Calum the approval.

"I give you my blessing. I want all of us to be still standing at the end of this."

"Sire!"

They all looked to the entrance of the library.

"Narum," Talum tried to joke, "you must have a thing for interrupting me while I am in the library."

"I . . . I was talking to Kesh."

Talum looked taken aback, but he did not challenge his words. It was just something that would take some getting used to.

"Speak," Kesh said. He'd recognized the young vampire as the one who had stolen the elixir from him when he and Talum had made the announcement to all of the Malum. It was then that Kesh took notice that Narum was just loyal to Talum. What he had done was nothing against Kesh personally; it was all for the sake of the long, drawn-out feud.

Narum's face held a look of alarm that spread throughout the room. Whatever he had to say was not good. "Sire, it's the Sefu. Word just got back from one of my human informants. It's the hunters. They are planning to attack at sunrise."

Chapter 15

Kesh hadn't been gone for more than an hour before Adirah got into a funk. She was missing her son, and now she was missing her love. Without them by her side, she felt empty. Surprisingly, the Malum made her feel very welcome and catered to all of her needs, the ones they could fulfill, anyway. Although Calum had offered to train her, Adirah made sure to sneak away before they were to head outside to the training course.

Her thoughts were consumed with questions. She felt like she didn't even know herself anymore. Everything had changed, and whenever she thought she finally had control, they changed again. And again. Now, whenever she looked in a mirror she would wonder if Kesh saw her, or Adie.

Adirah walked alone, offering kind smiles to any Malum she passed. She didn't know what the base of the feud was but, boy, was she glad that it was over. Between the Malum and the

Sefu, she didn't notice a difference besides
the name of their clans. Being around them
made her miss nothing about being human.
She'd lost her family a long time ago and, yes,
they crossed her mind, but not as much as they
used to.

"When this is all over I'm going to come
and visit you, Mom," she whispered to herself.
"Things have changed so much since the last
time you saw me. I hope my new appearance
doesn't freak you out."

"Your appearance would freak anybody out!"

Adirah rolled her eyes, recognizing the voice.
She kept walking without looking behind her,
hoping that her point would be taken. No such
luck.

"Aw, and here I am thinking that we made
such a good team."

"Didn't anyone ever teach you that it's not nice
to sneak up on people, Calum?"

"Yeah, of course." Calum grinned and appeared
at Adirah's side. "But I'm a vampire; there isn't a
lot of nice in anything I do."

"You're right," Adirah agreed and grew quiet.

"You're worried about Kesh, aren't you?" That
time when Calum spoke, her tone of voice was
softer.

"Yes," Adirah admitted. "I know this is something that he has to do alone, but I can't help it."

"You're supposed to be worried, you know that, right? If you weren't, I would have to tell Kesh that he needs to find himself a new queen."

"You wouldn't dare!"

"I'm just kidding." Calum nudged Adirah's arm with her own. "Look, if anybody understands you, it's me. All of this Ancient Lykan talk is scaring the shit out of me, and I have fought many Lykans in my time. But—"

"This is different?"

"Very."

"How so?"

"Well, for one, I've never fought a mega Lykan before." She paused so Adirah could laugh before she continued. "And two, I have never seen Talum this worried."

Adirah turned her head and studied the side of Calum's face. It dawned on her right then that maybe Calum hadn't followed her intentionally outside. Maybe she had to clear her mind of a few things too. Right then they both had one thing in common: they were both worried about the well-being of their men.

"Look, Calum, I'm sorry about, you know, kicking your ass last year," Adirah said and, just like she thought would happen, Calum's red lips spread into a wide smile. "But I'm glad that this has happened."

"I hope you don't think we're like best friends or something now." Calum's eyebrow raised.

"No, of course not!" Adirah linked arms with Calum and then slyly added, "But I've always wanted a sister."

Calum giggled and snatched her arm away. "Stop it!"

"Did you just giggle?" Adirah asked pretending to be shocked again. "A sense of humor is one thing, but I didn't think someone as tough as the great Calum was capable of giggling."

"I didn't used to always be this rock solid, you know."

"No, I didn't," Adirah said, and when Calum cut her eyes at her, she shrugged her shoulders. "Enlighten me."

"Talum would have never fallen in love with me if I were a bitch all the time. He wasn't always such a hard ass either. There was once a time when nothing mattered but our love for each other. When he first started the Malum, it was just supposed to be a place he called home. But he let his anger at Kesh consume him. He lost his way. I helped bring him back."

"Really?" Adirah gave Calum a knowing look.

"Okay, okay! I might have fueled the fire a little bit."

"A little bit?"

"Give me credit for something, Adirah."

"Okay, okay. I will let you have this one. But just this one."

"Thank you. I just realize now that we all have our own crosses to bear and we have always been stronger together than apart. There is room for only one king, and I'm happy that it's Kesh."

"You mean that?"

"Hell yes. Now I have Talum all to myself again!"

They both shared another laugh before sitting down under a tree facing the big house.

"Okay, I have to ask . . ." Adirah put her palms in the air, and Calum squinted at her.

"I don't want to hear any more of your jokes, Adirah. I have too much on my mind right now."

"No jokes, I swear. It's just . . . come on. Talum, Calum? That can't be your real name. It just can't be!"

"How do you figure it isn't?" Calum asked and looked out into the distance. "It could be, but you're right. It isn't."

"Soooo?" Adirah pressed when Calum didn't say anything after her statement.

"So what?"

"Tell me!"

"No."

"Why?"

"Because she died a long time ago."

"But if I'm correct, so did Calum."

Calum was shocked as she looked at the bold vampire woman next to her. She opened her mouth to say something mean, but she couldn't. What Adirah said was the truth. Calum was a vicious queen who would do anything to cause another pain. She was a person who was hurting and lost herself. Calum was the name of someone who did not know what she wanted; and, even though she still did not know where she was going, she was positive that she would never be Calum again.

"My name was . . . is Ceela."

"Ceela what?"

"Ceela That's All I'm Telling You. Pushy ass."

"All right, all right. I'll take it," Adirah said smiling. "Maybe I am a little pushy, so I'll back off for now. You know what?"

"What?"

"I always wanted a sister named Ceela."

Ceela punched Adirah softly in the arm, and the two of them fell back laughing with their eyes on the sky. Ceela's mind was on Talum, while Adriah's was on Kesh.

"Adirah?"

"Yeah?"

"Do you think that Kesh can really convince the Sefu that the Malum are their allies now? Without them seeing it for themselves? I mean, no offense, but Kesh did abandon them for a year. And our two clans have kind of had our differences. And I've heard things about these new hunters."

"What kinds of things?"

"They're more prepared for us than they've ever been. Narum says they can move like us and fight like us. I'm worried that the Sefu won't be expecting that."

"What are you saying?"

"I don't think we should wait for Kesh to return. I think the Malum should move out tonight."

Adirah sat up abruptly and leaned on her arm so that she could look down at Ceela. She looked for a trace of a smirk, but when she saw that Ceela was dead serious, she got completely to her feet.

"I couldn't agree with you more. Let's get everyone together to help the Sefu."

Chapter 16

It had been so long since Mezza walked the earth. He'd forgotten the smells and the sights in his seemingly forever slumber. Everything was different from what he remembered. It was all so overwhelming that he didn't leave the comforts of his home until his thirst was completely fed. He hadn't tasted flesh for centuries, and he filled up on it during the first five days of his awakening.

He barely slept because the only dreams he had were nightmares of his last memories. The battle with the Ancient vampires was one that they were supposed to win. In the beginning, it seemed as though victory would surely be theirs, but then things took a turn for the worse. He saw his brothers killed while he and Tidas became prisoners of a witch's spell. After he wiped out the vampires, he planned on going after the witch's coven. They would pay for what was done to them. However, now, his focus was on the one who had awakened him.

The curse was written in hopes that the loophole would never be broken, but with the birth of the baby vampire, it was. Mezza knew it was out there somewhere; he could smell it. It had to be killed along with anything else that had the means to destroy him. He refused to be locked away ever again; and once he found where his brother lay resting, the two would rule the world together.

"Sire?"

The voice interrupting his thoughts made Mezza come back to reality. He was in his usual spot in his room, gazing into the fire. He was expecting the young Lykan to return, so he'd kept his door slightly cracked. Although his back was to the Lykan, he could see him just with his senses.

"Did you bring what I asked?"

"Thirty human hearts? Yes, sire."

"Place them there." Mezza pointed his dark chocolate hand to the place beside his chair. "What are the others doing?"

"Training. The full moon is only one week away, sire. We are preparing for an all-out massacre."

"Have any new troops come to my door?"

"Yes. About ten more, earlier today. They heard your call and are ready to pledge their allegiance to you."

"Good." Mezza reached down and grabbed a heart from the bloody bucket the Lykan had set next to him. He brought it to his lips and took a big bite out of it. He savored the sweet taste on his tongue before he swallowed it. "Are there any women?"

"Yes," the young Lykan answered.

"It's been so long since I lay with a woman," Mezza stated feeling his human form getting warm all over. "Send only one to my room."

"As you wish."

In the time that it took for the woman to show up to his room, he'd already cleaned his hands and his face. When she walked in the room, Mezza was lying on his bed completely naked. His muscular frame was exposed, and so was his thick chunk of meat, standing at attention.

"Do not be afraid," Mezza told her, seeing the fear frozen on her face. "This is an honor. Are you hungry?"

"No, thank you. I just fed." Her voice was tiny, but he heard her two hearts beating loud and clear. She was strong, and he wanted to see how strong.

"Take your clothes off," he instructed, and she did it. "Slower. We are in no rush. What is your name?"

"Nara," she said, unsnapping her bra and releasing her full breasts.

His eyes watched her intently, lustfully. Her light caramel body was curved in all of the right places. He could smell her womanhood from there, and it made the beast in him hungry to be released. Once every article of her clothing was removed, he motioned for her to get on the bed with him.

"Nara," he growled in a low voice, "you are very beautiful. Show me what your mouth can do behind closed doors."

He watched her breasts bounce as she walked and he bared his teeth. He could sense that she liked the way he was watching her and she began to grow more confident in what she was doing. She got sexily on the gigantic bed and crawled sexily up to where he was. Before he could instruct her on how he liked things to be done, she arched her backside in the air as she licked his long shaft all the way up to the tip. Once there, she wrapped her full lips around the three inches of girth and worked her way down. Her mouth was so wet, and soon the room was filled with sounds of her choking on his manhood. His hands gripped the back of her disheveled short hair as he shoved himself deeper and deeper down her throat. He fucked her face with no mercy, barely giving her time to catch her breath.

He let go of her hair and let her do her own thing on him. She licked, kissed, and slurped until he let out one gasp after the other. He couldn't believe that he was sentenced to centuries of no pleasure. The night wasn't even over, and he knew he would have to reserve more time for his sexual appetite.

"Can I please get on it now?" Nara begged him. "I'm so wet between my legs. I want you to feel me."

Women had become bolder with their needs since the last time Mezza lay with a woman. Then, they were too prudish to tell you what they wanted. If they did, they would be perceived as a common whore. But Nara had no problem letting Mezza know how badly she wanted him inside of her, to which he had no objections.

Nara straddled him and slowly slid down on his thick ten inches. She hissed as he worked his way inside of her. She felt so tight to him, and he could barely keep his eyes open as she rode him. It felt like he was on the slipperiest slope, and he didn't want to get off.

"It's so big, sire. It's so big!"

Mezza opened his eyes so that he could see himself sliding in and out of her. He noticed that she was not coming all the way down on him and he shook his handsome head at her. He pulled her down toward him so that he could taste her light brown nipples.

"Mmmm, sire! Yes, fuck me and suck my titties. Yes! Like that."

She was so busy being pleasured by his tongue action she didn't even notice his grip around her waist grow tighter. He thrust up at her so suddenly her scream pierced his ears.

"Yes!" he growled as he thrust up again, fitting all of himself inside of her tight hole. "I told you not to be afraid. Take it. Your king says take it!"

"Yes, sire," she whimpered as he fucked her into oblivion.

It was like she was his property. She allowed him to do anything he wanted to do to her body. No hole or position was off-limits to him. He sexed her with so much power and authority that, by the time they were finished, she'd climaxed at least five times.

She tried to stand to leave, but she collapsed on the ground. Mezza stood up and scooped her into his arms and placed her on the bed.

"Rest," he told her. "You have pleased me greatly tonight. For that, you deserve to sleep."

She smiled weakly up at him and was passed out by the time he made his way back over to his chair. He'd released some of his pent-up frustration on Nara, but it was not even a quarter of it. His eyes fell back on the flicker of the flames, and he allowed his thoughts to consume him. All of that sexing had worked up an appetite for him. It was a good thing he had a bucket full of hearts to eat.

Chapter 17

"Do you think that he will succeed?"

Tep sat on the same bench as Dena as she watched the passageway. She'd been doing that since Kesh and Adirah left. There was no word of them or about whether they had succeeded. She hoped they were okay and hadn't run into any bumps in the road.

"I have much faith in Kesh."

"I don't see why. He reminds me of any other roughneck vampire his age."

"His age?" Dena couldn't help but chuckle. "Tep, you do realize that Kesh is centuries old."

"That doesn't matter. He's reckless!"

"You don't even know him."

"I know enough to say he's reckless!"

"How, for falling in love? Or for putting his family first?"

"For both."

"Tep."

"Okay, okay, okay. I guess he's not that bad."

"Not at all," Dena said thinking about Kesh's contagious smile. "Adie wouldn't have given her essence to just anyone. Not even for love. Kesh is special, and it is important that we keep him knowing as much."

"So then that answers my question."

"What question?"

"Do you think he will succeed?"

"Yes."

"Why?"

"Because he has to. The entire vampire race is depending on him. Plus, we have his son. If Kesh does not come back, it is because he can't, not because he does not want to."

"Then I will trust your judgment," Tep said after some seconds of silence. "What about her?"

"She is who I'm worried about. She needs more training. She is not ready for battle."

"They all will when they get here. We will need to prepare them all for what can and will happen. I can't help but wonder which one was awakened."

"Mezza or Tidas," Dena said shaking her head. "Both are monsters. It does not matter which one is awake right now. They both will suffer the same fate. Hopefully, Kesh comes back in the next day or two so that we can really prepare. We need the numbers, Tep. It is the only way we will survive this war."

"I know; there is strength in numbers. I just hope they are good enough."

"They will be. Two of the best warriors will be coming back with Kesh and Adirah."

"Who?"

"Calum and Talum, heads of the Malum clan. Soon to be stripped of their titles and made to follow only Kesh."

"Wait, did you say Calum?"

"Yes."

"Isn't that—"

"Yes."

"Wow. I thought she would be dead by now."

"No. She was turned a long time ago."

"She chose to leave?"

"Yes."

"And you let her?"

"Yes."

"Why?"

"I will not make anyone stay here who does not genuinely want to. This is a sanctuary for vampires, not a prison. Forcing people to stay here against their own will would make me no better than a human or a Lykan."

Tep nodded and looked back toward the passageway; they both did. After about five minutes Tep sighed and stood. He kissed Dena's hand before he departed, heading back toward the castle.

As he walked, he couldn't help but hope that they could all trust her belief in Kesh. The night of the full moon was nearing, and they were all preparing for war. Unless everyone was in position, they would all perish.

Chapter 18

Kesh, of course, had hoped that he would have a little more time to prepare. He had no idea what he would say to the Sefu when he appeared on their doorstep. He had abandoned them, and he knew they felt the same way. He left with no word of where he was going and if or when he was coming back. It would not be a happy reunion when he showed up, but he had run out of options. With the hunters on the move, he had no other choice. They would all die if he did not warn them about the upcoming attacks.

When Kesh had prepared to depart once again, Adirah had made plans to go with him. They were in the kitchen, along with Talum and Calum discussing their next moves. Talum had given Kesh a supply of blood that could last him two days' time and when Adirah saw that she raised her eyebrow.

"You're going alone?"

Kesh had known the question was coming, but he was prepared for it. Thas time he knew that Adirah could not come with him. It was something that he would have to do alone. The mistake he'd made last time was forcing his queen on his people without taking the time to consider how they felt about it. Regardless, he was going to do what he wanted with his life, but still, he thought about the way he was welcomed by the Ancients. The Sefu was his only family for so long and the least he could have done was ease their minds and make sure that they had faith in him. He was going to make it right. He had to.

"Yes, Dira. It's something that I have to do." Kesh readied himself for her rebuttal, but surprisingly it never came.

"I understand." Adirah walked to where he was standing beside the island. She stood close to him with her palms pressed on his chest and her eyes locked on him. "This is something that only you can do. If you leave now, you will make it before midnight. Just promise me something."

"What's that?"

"That you'll come back to me."

"There is no force on this earth that could keep me away from you." Kesh leaned in and kissed her cheek tenderly. "You are the love of my life."

Talum said, "While you are gone I will ready my clan. Some of them, I'm afraid, aren't taking the threat as seriously as they should. Some of them won't say it, but they are terrified. They aren't as old as the vampires in the Sefu and haven't seen or heard of anything like this."

"It's a bunch of hocus-pocus to them," Adirah said.

"Exactly. We need every number fighting now more than ever."

"Once we go to the Ancients' castle, everything will change."

"We will leave as soon as Kesh returns with the Sefu." Talum had walked up to Kesh and patted his back once with a strong hand. "So hurry, brother."

Now, the engine of the SUV purred lightly as Kesh turned the ignition off. The vehicle was parked outside of the place he'd called home for so long. Most of the lights inside were on, and he wondered if they were anticipating his arrival. With Tiev going ahead of him, he guessed that they were. There was no point in postponing the inevitable. Stepping out of the vehicle, Kesh began his short journey to the front door.

That time, he determined that sneaking in would cause too many problems. He would pay the Sefu the proper respect and come through the front door like he should. However, it was his home and, until stated otherwise, he was still king. So, knocking on the door was out of the question. His hand wrapped around the door handle and he twisted it open. He hadn't been inside of the frat house for a second before he was swarmed by a group of vampires.

"Sefu! I told you he would come!"

As Kesh's back was forced to the wall and his arms were restrained by his side, he recognized Tiev's voice booming. Kesh looked around the foyer of the home, looking at almost all of the Sefu. He did not take the time to analyze the looks in their eyes, simply because he already knew what to expect to see. They were angry with him, and they had a right to be, and Tiev was feeding off of it. Kesh could have easily thrown back the ones holding him, but his intent was not to hurt anyone there. Well, maybe one of them. Kesh cut his eyes toward Tiev, who was standing on the staircase, and flashed his fangs.

"Release me."

Although his gaze was on Tiev, his statement was for the vampire men holding him. When they hesitated and looked to Tiev to see what they should do, Kesh growled loudly.

"I am still your king! I said release me!"

That time they didn't hesitate. Once their grip loosened, Kesh snatched away and stepped toward Tiev. Never in the million years that Kesh was promised on earth would he have believed he would see the day that Tiev turned on him. Kesh thought about all of the moments they had shared as brothers. He wondered if they were real or if Tiev was plotting to replace him the whole time. He did not understand it, but he wanted to.

"We have fought together on the bloodiest of battlefields with only each other to depend on. I would give you the fangs out of my mouth if you needed them. Why have you betrayed me like this, Tiev?"

"Why do you think, Kesh?"

"Is this about Vila?" Kesh demanded to know. "Are you doing all of this because of her?"

Tiev quickly glanced at a female vampire in the large group before turning back to Kesh. "No. This has always been about me and you, Kesh. Do you think that this is something I wanted? Do you think that it pleasures me to have to let the Sefu see you in this kind of light? After all this time of being the right to your left hand, I started to realize that I was also your brain. If it weren't for me, this clan would have been done for long ago."

"In all of these years, I will admit that you have been an important part of the survival of the Sefu," Kesh started. "But if you think that providing aid to the king, the job you were appointed to do, qualifies you to throw me down from my throne and sit in it yourself, you are sadly mistaken. You have never done more than you were asked to do. You could never be king of this clan."

"Is that right? I've been doing a good job running things for the past year when you left us."

"And why did I leave, Tiev?"

Tiev was quiet as he gathered his thoughts.

"Tiev!" It was Kesh's turn to have a booming voice. "Why did I leave?"

Kesh's eyes cut at Tiev, and Tiev's mind went back to the night that he was sure to have killed Kesh. He remembered the rage that filled him at the time and the embarrassment of having to tell Talum that Kesh had gotten away. If the plan had gone the way he needed it to back then, the two vampires wouldn't even be having an exchange. Tiev would have been appointed king without an argument.

"You left because . . ." Tiev's voice faltered, and he looked around at all of the Sefu eyes on him. The truth was so far away from his mind that he almost believed the lies that were about to spill from his mouth. "He left because he did not want to be your king anymore! All he cares about now is that mortal girl he turned into one of us. Don't you see? He has replaced his family with a new one. He does not care about you. He only cares about himself."

The Sefu mumbled among themselves as they watched the exchange between their two leaders:

"Is that true?"

"Where is Adirah?"

"I don't trust him."

"Why did he come back now?"

"He's still our king."

While Tiev had done a good job protecting them and keeping them all alive the past year, that was only a year compared to the many they'd served under Kesh. Although skeptical about his motives, in all of the years they served him he had never done anything like that to them before. That could either work in his favor or be the thing that broke him.

"He is not your king!" Tiev told them. "I say we vote, and put this all to rest. This time, instead of a leader being designated to you, you will get to choose who you want to lead you."

That time Kesh took the time to look around at the house and the Sefu. Much had changed in the year he'd been gone. The staircase was no longer to the side, but now it wound in the middle of the foyer. Many of the photos that hung on the walls were gone and replaced with sick images of death. The color black was everywhere, giving the house an even darker vibe than it already had.

That wasn't the only thing. As he looked around at his people, it was apparent that they were divided in their own homes. They were grouped up together and looked like several small clans instead of one. Kesh felt that it was all his fault. He should have never brought violence to their front door and left them alone in the middle of it. That was not what a true leader would have done, and it made him wonder if they were better off without him. They whispered to each other and stared back at him with skeptical eyes. One by one, their heads began to nod in agreement with what Tiev was saying.

"If it is a vote that the Sefu want, it is a vote they will get," Kesh responded to their nods. "If you truly do not desire me as your king anymore, then I will step down as your king. You have an hour to make your choice; until then, I will be in my bedchamber. That is"—he cut his eyes at Tiev—"if your stand-in king has not made it his home yet."

Without another word or look to the Sefu, Kesh made his exit. He walked by the pretty vampire Tiev had looked at. When he was directly in front of her, Kesh offered her hard face a smile.

"Risa, beautiful Risa." Kesh chuckled and shook his head. "I understand why it is you Tiev has chosen to be by his side. Do you?"

"Because I will be a powerful queen," Risa said with naïveté.

"No, my sweet. You are naïve to his true nature. As you should be." Kesh shook his head and looked up to where Tiev stood staring back at him, most likely wondering what Kesh and Risa were discussing.

"He loves me."

"How can you be so sure?"

"He promised to make me queen."

"The Sefu already have a queen."

"And Tiev promised that she would perish along with you."

"Did he now? He also promised to remain loyal by my side for eternity."

"That is different. You left us!"

"Had I stayed, the love of your life would have continued to try to murder me. But I am back now. Now, again: do you know why it is you he has chosen?"

"He wants his equal by his side."

"Exactly. And you remind him of her, whether he will admit it or not. Vila was your creator, after all."

Kesh continued on his path, but not before he heard Risa sharply inhale at his words. Tiev had been working wonders at making the vampires around him truly believe that he cared about them. He didn't think about how all of his treacherous acts would affect the clan; all he was worried about was what position of power he would land in. Under Tiev's leadership, Kesh didn't see the Sefu lasting even another one hundred years.

Little did they know, now their fate was in their own hands. Kesh thought about telling them about the two great dangers coming their way at that very moment but, without their trust, they wouldn't believe him. The only reason he'd agreed to the vote was because it was the fastest way back into their graces.

"Enjoy your last seconds of comfort, Kesh," Tiev spat in a voice that only Kesh could hear as he went by. "Once I am appointed king, you will be banished from the Sefu and punished by death if you ever come back."

Kesh studied Tiev's face. He saw nothing but hatred there. He was certain that Tiev was upset that, although he'd been gone for a year, the

Sefu still treated him with respect. He must have expected them all to attack him upon arrival. What Tiev didn't understand was that, through the centuries of serving as the Sefu king, the bond he'd built with his clan was not that of a leader and his subjects. It was more of a father with his children. Their hesitance did not come from hatred or resentment; it came from hurt.

"When I, Kesh of the Sefu, remain king, Tiev, there will not be a vampire on this earth who can protect you. Nor will there be a fortress that you will be able to hide in."

Chapter 19

While the other vampires deliberated with each other, Kesh made it his business to travel the house to clear his head. He'd been there for less than an hour, but every second that went by was a waste. Sunrise grew nearer and nearer. He sighed as he maneuvered alone through the hallways of the second floor. His mind went back to the Ancients' castle and how, in days, it had become more of a home than his own. Nothing was familiar to him. In halls that he must have walked hundreds of times, he felt like a stranger. He stopped randomly and looked over his shoulder.

"I know you are following me. What do you want?"

From the shadows, Risa materialized. She wore a pair of jeans and a silk blue blouse with a pair of comfortable boots. She eyed him curiously, her expression a lot softer than before. It was true: she'd been following him the second he stepped out of his bedchamber.

"I'm sorry."

"Are you? Your strong scent that lingers in my bedchamber says otherwise. Why are you here? I don't think Tiev would be too happy if he knew we were speaking right now."

"Because I want to know why you have returned. Why now?"

Kesh heard her question but didn't answer her. He kept walking and, just like he thought she would, she appeared at his side.

"Is that what you have gotten good at doing? Walking away?"

"You wouldn't understand if I told you right now."

"I'm sorry," she said sarcastically. "When would be a better time? Maybe you could pencil me in. Kesh, our people are lost. More lost than they have ever been. The only thing that has made sense to them in the past year is Tiev, and now—"

"Now what?"

"Now I'm starting to feel as if he was the wrong person to put our trust in. Am I not right to feel like this?"

"He is the one you lie with every night. If you feel that way, then you are right."

"If I am right, then that means there is another meaning to your return. It isn't to just knock Tiev from the throne. You have never been a being to run off of his ego, so I will not stop until you answer me!"

Risa was relentless, just like he remembered. He stopped and faced her, like an equal. At first, he had been wary of making her into one of them. She was created with too much hatred and resentment in her heart. But soon she turned that hatred into love of a new family: the Sefu. He smiled to himself thinking of the day a hundred years ago that Vila turned her.

Winter was cold in Nebraska. Colder than any state that Kesh had ever traveled to. He and Vila were bundled up in long coats, boots, and scarves. He and Vila had traveled there together in response to news of a couple of rogue Lykans wreaking havoc throughout the state. The last thing they needed were any more eyes on their underground world, and they knew that the problem needed to be handled immediately. The werewolves were being smart about their hunts and only hitting the poverty-stricken parts of the state.

"The hunted become the hunters." Vila smirked at Kesh as they entered the last known area that the Lykans were in. "How ironic."

The night sky cloaked them as they walked side by side. In the distance, they heard shrieks and the cries of an attack happening.

"They need to be stopped. Too much blood has been being shed," Kesh said, and Vila raised her eyebrow at him.

"You say that like you care about the human lives they are destroying."

"Humans are nothing but cattle to our kind," Kesh said. "But sometimes even cattle deserve a chance at life."

"So, what about when you go hunting?"

Vila did not know that Kesh had been slowing down on killing his mortal prey. He often thought back to Adie and how she'd fought for humans. He felt as if he was going against what she stood for by killing them all the time. It wouldn't happen overnight, but sooner or later Kesh would come up with a system to feed without killing his victim.

Instead of telling Vila all that was on his mind, he grinned her way and shrugged his shoulders. "When I hunt, I make it a fair chance."

"Sure you do." Vila chuckled, but the smile quickly washed from her face. "Just don't do that tonight."

They turned down a block, and both stopped instantly. Almost two hundred feet in front of them, they saw the two beasts in the streets with their prey. The screams had stopped, and when Kesh's eyes graced each house on the block, he saw why. Every door was open, and blood smeared the concrete on the outsides of the homes. Laid out in the streets, sidewalks, and against cars were the dead bodies of the people on the block. Men, women, and children had been viscously slain, and most of their hearts were missing.

Suddenly, one of the Lykans stopped eating the brains of the elderly man in its claws and put its nose in the air. It sniffed once and threw the body to the side. Jumping up, it turned to face Vila and Kesh with a loud howl. The other followed suit and crouched low, preparing for battle.

"Kesh," Vila said with warning in her voice.

"On it."

The two of them threw their coats off and allowed for their bodies to transform. Kesh felt his muscles grow bigger and his fingers turn to claws. Once in their complete vampire form, the two of them ran full speed toward the beasts. Kesh took the one on the right, and Vila took the one on the left. They fought the beasts with no mercy, drawing blood from all over.

"Ahhhh!" Vila's battle cry filled the night air as her hand made its way into her opponent's back and yanked out its spine.

It dropped instantly, dead. With one still standing, Kesh's claws slashed ferociously at its face. Soon it was so covered in blood that the beast could not see. It began lashing out at nothing but air, missing Kesh every time. Kesh used that to his advantage and attacked every opening the beast had.

"Stop playing with it!" Vila called from off to the side. She'd gone back to grab their coats after she'd killed her Lykan and she was watching him battle. "Just kill it already."

Kesh put his hand around the beast's neck and held it up in the air. It was weak, and as his claws tried to remove Kesh's hand from around its neck, it slowly turned back into a human.

"What is your name?" Kesh asked the naked man now in his clutches. He loosened his grip slightly so that his question could be answered.

"I was so hungry. So thirsty. I could smell their blood. I wanted it."

"What is your name?" Kesh asked again.

"Willeth," he stuttered.

"Who turned you, Willeth?"

"I don't know his name. I don't even know what I am."

"You are a monster."

"And what are you?"

Their eyes locked for a second, right before Kesh went to crack his neck. He, however, didn't get the chance to. The sound of gunshots filled the air, and a gust of angry shouts followed them:

"Oh, my God! Dortha Jean!"

"Auntie Mable!"

"What happened? Who would do something like this? Oh, my God. Call the police! Somebody please just call the police!"

Kesh was caught so off guard that the young Lykan was able to slip through his fingers. He tried to go after him, but Vila snatched his arm and handed him his coat.

"We have to get out of sight!"

They moved quickly and were gone before anyone even knew they were there. There was an alley behind a row of houses, and they used it to head back to the main road.

"Don't come near me. I know what you are!"

The voice came from behind two tall metal trashcans. Kesh's eyes landed on a young woman who had been wounded badly. Her thick hair was pinned back into a ponytail, and the brown skin on her face had snow all over it. She wore only a dress, which looked like it would be very pretty had it not been for the blood smeared all over it. Her leg was twisted

at a grotesque angle, and it looked as if a chunk
was missing from it. She shivered as she cradled
a small child in her arms. Kesh could hear only
one heart beating, so he already knew the child
was dead. When they didn't stop, the girl pulled
a gun out on them and aimed it their way with
a shaky hand.

"I said stop!"

"We aren't going to hurt you," Kesh tried to
say soothingly with his hands up. "We are just
trying to go home.

"I know what you are!"

"Do you now?" Vila said, laughing slightly at
the sight of the gun. "And what are we?"

"Werewolves! She has blood all over her face!"

Kesh and Vila looked at each other and
shrugged their shoulders.

"Close," Vila said. "But not quite."

She flashed her fangs at Risa, who in return
jumped at the sight and emptied the gun's
entire clip into Vila. Kesh watched as Vila's
body jerked from the impact of each bullet,
but she did not fall. Her feet stayed planted
where they were and when Risa was done, she
stretched her neck from side to side. Risa's
eyes bulged out of her head as she watched the
bullets come back out of Vila's body and fall to
the ground. Vila's body healed right before her,
and she clutched the child's body even tighter.

"You're a vampire?"

"Yes," Kesh answered her.

"Before today, I never thought monsters existed!" Risa clenched her eyes shut. "I never thought they were real."

"What happened here?" Kesh asked her.

When she hesitated, Vila nodded and prompted her. "It's okay."

"My family and I, we were eating dinner, and there was a knock on the door. There was a man none of us had ever seen before. He was big, bigger than any man I have ever seen. He had hair all over his face like he didn't care to shave it off. At first, I thought he just had the wrong house. But then I heard the screams of our neighbors. I tried to call the police, but in this neighborhood, they wouldn't have shown up until tomorrow. And then . . . and then he changed into a beast. It slaughtered my entire family. My little sister." She put her head down on the child's body and sobbed. "It killed my sister!"

Vila knelt down next to the girl and put a hand softly on her shoulder. "What is your name?"

"Clarisa," she answered. "Please just leave me alone. Please, I have nothing left. You are all monsters."

"Yes," Vila started in a soft tone. "We are all monsters, but we are the lesser of the two evils. Tell me something, Clarisa: were you bitten?"

"No." Clarisa shook her head. "One of those things clawed a chunk of my leg away. I can't feel it anymore."

Kesh and Vila exchanged a look. She hadn't been bitten, which meant she wouldn't turn into a werewolf. Kesh knew what Vila was thinking but, before he could oppose, Vila's attention was already back on Clarisa.

"How old are you?"

"I just turned twenty-one at the beginning of December."

"If we leave you here like this, you will die. Do you know that?"

The girl slowly nodded.

"Well, Clarisa, how would you like to be twenty-one for eternity?"

"But what about Clara?" Clarisa kissed the forehead of her dead sister.

"Clara is already dead. Everyone is dead, but we can give you the opportunity to live."

Clarisa looked down once more at her sister. Her lips had already begun to turn blue. She was gone. Clarisa knew that she would soon meet the same fate if she didn't give in to the vampire in front of her.

She parted her trembling lips. "What is your name?"

"Vila."

"Will you take care of me, Vila?"

"Yes." Vila nodded. "Sefu take care of each other. Forever."

Kesh snapped back to reality and looked to Risa walking beside him. He never knew why Vila had taken a quick liking to Risa, but he thought it had something to do with the fact that she shot her. Ever since, she had done nothing but proven her loyalty to the Sefu, which was why he could not blame her for siding with Tiev. To her, it must have seemed like Kesh was the bad guy in the problem and Tiev was the only one trying to fix it.

"Everything must look so different to you," Risa said finally.

"What has happened since I have been gone?"

"A lot. The entire clan is divided."

"I would be telling lies if I said that I didn't notice that. When I walked in, my own clan reminded me of the cliques of college students on the campus. Why have they divided like this?"

"They've forgotten their common interests and only care about their own."

"Why have they remained here?" Kesh asked, but it was Risa's turn to ignore his question.

"Tiev said that we are vampires; therefore, we should live as such. He said we were growing too accustomed to living like humans."

"The purpose is to blend in as much as possible. Especially with everything that has taken place."

"Not according to Tiev. He said that was even more of a reason the Sefu need to spread in numbers."

"Spread in numbers?"

"Yes. Tiev has been making rogue vampires left and right. The only thing is, they are too reckless to commit to the ways of a clan. They do not want to follow the rules of the vampire; they just want the power."

"What happens to them when they do not want to be a part of the Sefu?"

"Tiev disposes of them."

"So, all in all, it is a waste of time," Kesh said and shook his head. He finally decided to address her question. "I came back because great danger is headed our way. Tiev is not a fit leader for the Sefu. Nor is he the type of general who would lead us well into battle."

"What?"

"Hunters, Risa. Hunters will infiltrate the Sefu clan at sunrise."

"How do you know this?"

"I was at the Malum estate earlier today."

"What!"

"It is not what you think." He went on to explain what all had happened in the past year. He didn't stop until it was all out and she was looking at him with a bewildered expression.

"Talum has stepped down as king?"

"Yes."

"And the human Adirah brought to our home last year has now become a hunter?"

"Yes."

"And the vampire she had relations with told you they were going to attack us at sunrise?"

"Pretty much."

"Okay, we're going to touch on the whole 'golden child' and 'Ancient vampire' things later. First things first: why haven't you warned the Sefu about the hunters?"

"They do not trust me anymore. This vote will allow me to address them as a whole."

"But will it be enough?" Risa studied the side of Kesh's handsome face to find an answer that did not come from his lips. She sighed. "You have always had the best poker face, Kesh. What about Tiev?"

Kesh had also told Risa about Tiev's betrayal. Listening to his words felt like a gut blow. Still, she couldn't say that she was surprised. He wasn't the same vampire she'd once known. She had never seen him so thirsty for power; and to know that he'd been in cahoots with the Malum the entire time, she knew there were no lengths to which he would not go.

"Even though now you say that the Malum are on our side, he will never stop attacking you. For all we know he will go to the Lykans next."

"Do you love him?"

"I thought I did." Risa looked down at the ground and felt her head shake from side to side. "But it seems that the vampire I loved never existed. I have a strong following here. He used me to get the clan on his side. He has to be stopped."

"Then help me."

It was at that moment another vampire woman appeared in front of them. She moved fast, and when Kesh saw who it was, he smiled. "Cera."

"Sire. I mean, King. I mean . . . Kesh?"

"You can call me whatever you like, my child."

Cera was one of the youngest vampires in the Sefu at only eighty years old. It had taken her a while to get used to life as a vampire, but she was one whom Kesh had always kept an eye on. She was only eighteen when she was turned, so her physique was that of a young girl. Kesh was the one who turned her as she lay dying of cancer.

He gave her life when the world around her was draining it out of her. He was the one who trained her and took her under his wing like she was a true daughter. It wasn't until Adirah came along that he stopped spending as much time with her.

"We are ready for you. In the basement."

"Of course," Kesh said and smiled. "You have grown stronger. I'm proud."

Cera nodded at Kesh and turned her back to him so that she could head back the way that she came. Unseen to Kesh, a broad smile spread across her face as she departed. Risa, however, noticed it and turned to face Kesh.

"You asked why the Sefu have remained, although divided in their own home?"

"Yes."

"Because of you."

"Me?"

"Despite the fact that you left without a good-bye, and despite their anger with you, to them, you are the only one who has ever offered any of our lives meaning."

"'Our'?"

"Yes." Risa nodded. "Including mine. We have allowed Tiev to step in from the shadows, but deep down we have all hoped that you would return. There is no other leader for the Sefu. They just need you to remind them."

Chapter 20

The day after the first vampire battle Ramel and Lina had fought together, he took her back to her home and asked her to come with him. He was sure that she was going to go running, but she didn't. She dived in even deeper. She didn't fully understand what she was getting herself into, but she said yes. She packed everything that she could and hit the road with Ramel without a second thought.

The hunter headquarters was in Georgia at an undisclosed location. The facility looked to be something out of a movie.

"This place looks like a military base," Lina said as they drove up to the tall gate.

"It's something like it. The government funds us."

"What? They know about these things?"

Ramel was shocked that she was so taken aback. He rolled his window down and showed the man at the window his badge.

"Commander, nice to have you back. Who is this you have with you?" The man, who looked to be in his early thirties, eyed Lina with his dark brown eyes. Lina read his suspicion but kept quiet.

"This is Lina; she is new on the job. Spread the word. I expect everyone to make her feel welcome and at home."

"Yes, sir." With that, the gate opened, and they drove through.

Ramel turned back to Lina. "Of course they know about the creatures of the underworld."

"Then why haven't they said anything?"

"Can you imagine the state of panic if everyone knew there were vampires, werewolves, and witches roaming the world?"

"Witches?"

"Yes. And if everyone knew about these things there would be so much chaos that no money would be made. And we all know what that means, so the Legion for Darkness division was created."

"Legion for Darkness?"

"Hunters. Why do you think the president crafted such a heavy military budget?"

Lina was quiet as they drove around the base. Finally, they stopped and parked outside a building that was bigger than the rest.

"This is where I live," he told her. "Only people on my team are permitted access to this building. The other hunters either live on base or, at their own risks, in their own homes."

"Who is on your team?"

"Come see."

Ramel took the keys out of the ignition and grinned at her before he got out of the vehicle. He grabbed her bags from the back and led her to the steel door of the building.

"It smells like—"

"Garlic."

"Yes." Lina turned her nose up. "Lots of garlic."

"Well, get used to it. Everything in this place is doused in it."

"Great," Lina said under her breath when Ramel opened the door. "Just great."

"The basement is where we train." Ramel pointed to a hallway that led to an elevator. "We have all types of stuff down there. You can get to it through that elevator, or the ones closer to the west wing. This floor is more of a—"

"Rec hall."

"How did you know?"

"I don't knowww." She shrugged. "The arcade games and card table might have given it away. Or maybe the big yellow plush chairs with the bookshelves next to them. Orrrr, it could have been the glass windows around the pool."

"Touché." Ramel laughed again. "Let's go upstairs. I'll show you where you will be staying. If you are staying, that is."

Lina heard the hint of a question in his voice, but she wasn't in the state to answer him. She didn't know what she was going to do. A year ago if she would have tried to think that far out, she would have only been able to picture herself in a classroom. Now there she was in the middle of a specially designated military base with the leader of vampire hunters.

She followed closely behind Ramel and took notice that the smell of garlic wasn't as bad inside as it was outside. She guessed that was because if anything was ever able to make it inside, they were all trained to handle the problem. The upstairs was shaped in a square and, no matter where you were in the hallway, you could look down at the rec room.

"This place reminds me of a hotel I stayed in once."

"Well, it's very different from a hotel, trust me." They reached the room that he was going to make hers. "Here we are. Now—"

"Commander! You weren't going to tell us you were back?"

"Yeah, we had to hear from the gate that you arrived."

"This must be the newbie. Looks kind of small, don't you think?"

Lina and Ramel turned to face the three newcomers. They all looked to be fit and in shape, even the woman. To Lina's far right, one man was tall and had muscles on top of muscles. His hair was cut into a faded flattop, and on his roasted caramel–colored face there was a thick scar on his left cheek. He had a gap between his front teeth, and his eyes matched his complexion.

The woman, in the middle, was of average height and had very light brown skin and curly hair. Her eyes were the color of sand, and her teeth were white and straight. Her pretty face had been hardened, and Lina wondered if she knew how to smile.

The last man, on Lina's left, wasn't tall but he wasn't short, either. He stood at about five foot seven and wore his hair in four neat braids.

"Meet my team," Ramel said with a wide smile. "From the left, this is Clem, Mims, and Tiger. Team, this is Lina. She's going to be joining us for a while."

"Since when have you brought back the women you bag?" Mims asked.

Lina cut her eyes at the girl. She had some nerve. She was also the one who had made the comment about Lina's size.

"The only thing we bagged were the ashes of the vampires we killed together," Lina snapped. "The ones you think I'm too small to handle."

"Oooh, looks like Mims has herself a challenger."

Tiger and Clem slapped hands as they laughed at the scene taking place in front of them, but they stopped once they saw Ramel's face.

"That wasn't appropriate, Mims," Ramel told her with ice in his tone.

"Sorry, sir. I joke with all of the guys like that," Mims replied. "I didn't mean to offend your little girlfriend." Mims didn't wait for Ramel to address her again. Instead, she glared at Lina one last time and took her leave.

"Don't mind her, Lina," Ramel said in an apologetic tone.

"Yeah, she's been on edge like that ever since we lost Abe," Tiger said, backing him up.

"Lost?"

"He was killed on our last mission," Ramel said and balled his hands into fists. "I should have—"

"Not with this again! Commander, there was nothing that you could have done," Clem told him. "He ran into that building after you gave us a direct order."

"I could have gone after him."

"And been killed yourself? No. Abe signed his own death warrant. His thirst for glory landed him in an early grave. You had no control over that."

"You're right."

Although that was what his words said, Lina could tell by his tone and expression that he did not really feel that way. She studied him until his eyes found hers, and he straightened up.

Lina found her voice. "It was nice to meet you guys. Hopefully, Mims comes around and I can say the same about her."

"You too, but I have a question for you, if you don't mind me asking," Clem said.

"Yes?"

"Where are you coming from?"

"Charlotte, North Carolina."

"Before you met our commander, had you ever seen a vampire?"

"Yes. They attended my college."

Tiger and Clem exchanged confused glances.

"I attended the historically black college there and toward the end of the school year I learned that one of the frat houses was inhabited by a clan of vampires. The Seafood clan or something."

Ramel, who had just opened the door to Lina's room, stopped in his tracks. His eyes widened and his head whipped to her. Yes, she had told him about a group of vampires at her college, but not once did she mention that they were the Sefu clan.

"The Sefu? Lina, do you mean the Sefu clan?"

"I mean, I guess." Lina almost took a step back at the way they were staring at her. She didn't know what their deal was and she suddenly wished she had kept her mouth shut.

"You know the location of the Sefu clan?" Clem asked. "We have been trying to locate them for years."

"And you mean to tell me that after all this time they have been right under our nose? Posing as kids in college?" said Tiger.

"What is so special about the Sefu clan?" Lina asked.

"They are the strongest of all vampire groups. We call them the elites. There is another known as the Malum. Any others are undocumented and rogue," said Clem.

"We will discuss this more later," Ramel said and dismissed them with his eyes.

"Okay, Commander. We're going to go check on Mims."

When they left, Lina was finally able to step foot inside the place she might be calling home. On the outside, she thought she would be stepping into a bunker with metal walls. But once inside she felt like she was in an elegant master bedroom. The walls were a deep red, and the queen-sized bed had a tan comforter with pillows to match.

"This bed looks softer than any I've ever sat on. And this carpet probably feels like heaven under my toes," Lina said in awe.

Ramel set her bags on the computer chair and showed her where everything was. She even had a fully stocked fridge and a television, with all of her favorite channels, hanging on the wall. "You wouldn't have to leave your room unless you wanted to. Or unless there was a mission."

"I see that," Lina said sitting down on the bed. It was as comfortable as she thought.

"I mean, of course I would want you to. I mean, to get comfortable with the team, of course," Ramel said, stumbling over his words.

"Uh-huh." Lina smiled at how flustered he looked. "Anyways, what's her deal?"

"Whose deal?"

"Mims."

"Oh, Mims is just Mims." Ramel shrugged his shoulders but didn't look at her.

"Hmmm."

"What does that mean?"

"You won't look at me, and it seems like there is more to the story, that's all. You don't have to talk about it if it's awkward."

"It's not awkward; it's just complicated."

"How so?"

"You know how some things that happen aren't meant to happen?"

"Yes." Lina nodded, thinking about what had transpired between herself and Narum.

"Well, me and Mims was something that happened that wasn't meant to."

"I knew you two had a fling. It's so obvious." Lina rolled her eyes at Ramel.

"I wouldn't call one time a fling."

"Once?"

"Okay, twice. But that's it, I swear. It was never anything more than that, but now I think her feelings have gotten involved."

"I mean, you can't blame her. You're very handsome," Lina teased. "With your dimples and sexy lips. You're the type of man any girl would go crazy for."

"What about you?"

"What about me?"

"Am I the kind of guy you would go crazy for?"

Lina was stumped by his question, mainly because she didn't expect it to come out of his mouth. Her lips parted and closed a few times before she finally smirked and cocked her head.

"Maybe, but I usually don't date guys with weird jobs like vampire hunting, or who drink stuff that gives them magical powers."

"Oh, yeah?" Ramel laughed and backed out of the room. "Whatever. Get settled and come find me in the meeting room. You can't miss it; it's right next to the pool."

"Okay," Lina said.

Ramel shut the door behind him, happy that the exchange hadn't been as weird as he thought it would be. Now the only thing that was on his mind was that they had the key to the Sefu location in the same place as them. The time to make a move was now or never.

When he reached the lower level of the building, he saw his three team members already huddled up. When Mims saw him, she instantly cut her eyes but didn't say anything.

"Is she all right?" Clem asked. He had always been the caring one out of all of them. If anyone was the glue to keep them all together, it was Clem.

"Yeah, she's doing good."

"Perfect, because she is somebody we need to keep happy."

"How do you know that she's telling the truth about knowing their location?" asked Mims.

"She said 'Seafood clan' instead of Sefu," Tiger told her. "She didn't even know the importance of the information she was giving us. She wasn't lying."

"Okay, so now what?"

"We attack," Ramel told her matter-of-factly.

"Attack? Attack who? A whole clan of vampires who are skilled in killing people like us? Next plan."

"Mims!"

"No, Tiger, you know I'm right. We haven't even been on a mission since Abraham's dumb ass got himself killed. And we have never gone on a mission with a newbie so soon, Ramel, and you know it."

"She's good."

"She may have been good with you, but how do you know she is a good fit for this team? That is what we are, right? Or is this the Ramel show?"

Tiger and Clem were quiet as they watched the exchange. It was no secret that the commander and Mims had allowed lust to intervene with the boundaries of their positions. Now it was all coming out. From the moment Mims laid eyes on Lina, her claws were out.

"Mims, come talk to me in private," Ramel said.

"No. Whatever you need to say to me, you can do it right here."

"Okay." Ramel looked her squarely and hard in the eyes. "What happened between us was just sex. I fucked you, okay? We didn't make love, we are not in a relationship, and we will never be that close again. You are my soldier, so when I tell you to jump you ask me how gotdamn high. When I tell you to shoot, you ask which way to aim. And when I tell you we are going into battle you suit the fuck up. Do I make myself clear?"

Mims's eyes were so wide that they looked like saucers. There was a hint of water, but she did not let a tear drop. Her mouth pressed into a straight line, and she nodded.

"I said, do I make myself clear, soldier?"

"Yes, sir."

"Good. Now I need more soldiers prepped. We will attack as soon as we are ready. Mims, since you are so afraid of her not being ready, I will leave it to you to give her the best training that you can."

Days passed. The night before the big attack finally came upon them, Ramel found himself in Lina's doorway watching her prepare. She was beautiful. He'd always thought that about her. He tried not to let it get in the way of him doing his job, but there was something about her that he could not shake.

He cleared his throat so that she would know he was there, but she still never looked up.

"I've been watching you stand there staring at me for the last two minutes."

"Has it been that long?"

"Maybe I am wrong: five minutes."

"You have jokes." Ramel chuckled and stepped inside, closing the door behind him. "We need that around here. I feel that everyone has lost their sense of humor."

"I mean, look at what you guys do for a living. It would be hard to find humor in that."

"Still, this is the life they will live for the rest of their lives. Why not find happiness and laughter somewhere? If not, they're risking having to live a miserable life."

"I guess you're right."

"I'm always right."

"Okay, Mr. Always Right, tell me what else you know."

"I know that you love that vampire you let get away." Ramel knew he was reaching, but he needed to know. Not needed, but wanted to know, for the sake of the mission, and a little for his own peace of mind.

"Definitely didn't love him. I barely knew him."

"But you slept with him."

"Hey, I was in college. Everybody was sleeping with everybody."

"I'm not joking, Lina."

"Okay." Lina sighed and faced him with her hands on her hips. "Fine. His name is Narum and, no, I didn't love him. But I liked him. I thought he was different from the other boys at the college."

"So you slept with him because you liked him a lot?"

"No, I just liked him." Lina rolled her eyes. "What, Ramel? Do you want to know the details of our sexual relationship? Do you want to know how nasty I was with him? Do you want to know what my screams sound like when I'm coming?"

Ramel felt like he had pressed too hard. He no longer had control of the conversation, and he found himself gulping with each word that came out of her mouth. She was turning him on because, yes, he did want to know all of those things. He couldn't shake the fact that a vampire had been with such a beautiful person. And the way they had looked at each other before Lina let him go lit in his stomach a fire that he didn't even know existed. He was jealous, and he couldn't help it.

Before he knew it, he was so close to her that her breasts were on his chest. His hands found their way to her waist. He grabbed her lightly at first, but when she didn't push him off of her, he cupped her ass in his hands.

"Did you put your mouth on him?" he heard himself ask and Lina shook her head. "Can I put my mouth on you?"

"Yes," Lina breathed.

Their first kiss sent tingles to her toes. It had been so long since she'd been with a man. She just wanted to pour herself into him. Her body melted against his and she wrapped her arms around his shoulders to pull him closer. Their tongues danced like old friends as they kissed each other hungrily. Her hands found the buckle to his pants, wanting to skip through the fore-play.

"Are you sure?" he asked when he pulled back from her.

"I might not be alive tomorrow. So just make me come hard, okay?"

She stepped back from him and stripped out of her clothes. When she was completely naked, she rubbed her erect nipples before climbing on the bed, giving him the perfect view of her shaved pussy.

"You're nasty," Ramel whispered when she finally rested on her back and put her legs in the air. Her middle finger slowly circled around her swollen clit, and that made his own private part expand in his underwear. "Real nasty."

He unzipped his pants the rest of the way and let them and his underwear drop to the floor. Stepping out of them, he removed his shirt as well, wanting to feel her bare breasts against his skin while he sexed her. When he climbed onto the bed, he started in between her thighs. He kissed, sucked, and nibbled her skin until he finally made his way to his true destination. He could tell that she was already moist, but he wanted to make her wetter. Nudging her hand out of the way, he began to go to work on her. He placed her engorged button between his lips and sucked on it like he was trying to get juice from a straw while he placed two fingers in her love canal. Her body twisted and turned, but she didn't run from the pleasure he was giving her, and he liked that. When he felt her jerk slightly, and he heard the first loud moan escape her mouth, he released her clit from between his lips and let his tongue beat the orgasm out of it.

"Ramel!" Lina's cry filled the air. "It feels soooo good! I'm coming, baby!"

Ramel licked up as much of the stream that shout out as he could, but he couldn't take it anymore. He wiped his face off and mounted her. She hadn't seen the ten inches that he was packing, so she wasn't prepared for the damage he was about to do to her walls.

"When I put this dick in you, don't run," he whispered in her ear as he caressed her nipples. "We're about to practice for this battle. You aren't going to run away from battle, are you?" He put the tip of his manhood at her opening and forced it in.

"Hsssss," she hissed and tensed up under him.

"Nope, open those legs. You're running from me." Ramel let her breasts go and grabbed her wrists instead. Placing them at the sides of her head, he looked down into her face. "Are you going to run away in battle?"

"Nooooo!"

At that moment he forced a little more in. She was so tight he was loving it. "I'm so sorry," Ramel whispered and kissed her lips. "I don't want to hurt this pussy. I really don't. She's so tight, and he's so big. I'm sorry."

Lina sucked her breath in and opened her legs as wide as they could go. Her eyes locked on Ramel's and she nodded, giving him the okay. "Put him all in, Commander. I won't run from battle. Sometimes in war, there will be casualties."

He was completely turned on. He did as she said, and forced the rest of him inside of her.

After a few powerful thrusts, her screams of pain turned into whimpers of pleasure. She had told him the truth when she said that she wouldn't run because, after a while, she was throwing it back at him.

"Catch this dick, baby. Catch it," he moaned in her ear.

She was as hungry for him as he was for her. Lina pushed him off of her so that she could straddle him. She sucked her teeth as she came down on him, but soon her wetness had her sliding up and down on him easily.

"Uh! Uh! Uh! Uh!" she moaned loudly as she bounced. "Ramel! Ramel! Oh, my God, Ramel. It's so big. Why is it so big? Why are you doing this to me?"

Ramel gripped her hips and guided her. He let her talk to herself as he watched her breasts bounce. After a while, he grew tired of her being in control and held her in place so that he could thrust up into her. He granted her no mercy; he needed to go as deep as he could. He was going so fast that all she could do was gasp and throw her head back. Her second orgasm snuck up on her, and her body shook viciously. Her juices ran down his shaft and onto his torso, and he licked his lips.

"Turn around," he commanded.

She was still shaky, but she managed to do as he said. She put her chest on the bed and her head on the pillow. Her arch was perfect and gave Ramel the perfect access. When she felt him slide into her swollen box again, she bit her lip and turned her nose up as if she smelled something foul.

"Mmmmmm," she moaned. "If I had known it was this good I would have already done this."

"Me too, baby," Ramel moaned slapping her ass. "Me too!"

She was beautiful, strong, smart, and had gold between her legs. He didn't see himself letting her go anywhere anytime soon. Ramel pounded into her until he couldn't hold it in anymore and the two of them climaxed together. When he pulled out of her, they both collapsed on the bed. He kissed her deeply in hopes of showing her she was more than just a quick fuck.

"That was the best sex I've ever had," Ramel told her honestly. "You are a certified freak."

"Don't start stalking me."

"Too late; and now you stay in my house. Girl, I'm going to be at your door every night!"

Lina swatted him playfully and fell into a fit of giggles. "You are silly."

"A little bit. I told you that we can find laughter in this life, didn't I?"

"You did," she whispered weakly. "Is any of this real?"

"All of it is real."

"I feel so safe with you," she said and lay her head on his chest. "I just want to stay in this moment forever."

"You can," he said and kissed her forehead. *After I kill Narum, yes, you can.*

Chapter 21

Risa made sure to enter the basement a few minutes before Kesh. She did not want Tiev to have the suspicion that she was just with him plaguing his mind. Everything that was once in the basement had been cleared out to make room for the chairs that now faced the front of the basement. Most of the Sefu were already there, and Tiev shot a confident smile her way, and she gave him her most believable one back. Cloaking her thoughts as best she could, she found a seat near the front.

"This should be interesting," she murmured to herself.

"Yes, it shall."

Risa looked up to see Cera take the seat next to her, and the two vampire women exchanged a look. After a few moments, they both turned to face the front until all of the seats were filled.

"Where is Kesh?" Cera asked.

"He's coming," Risa assured her. "He didn't come back to run away again."

"I hope not."

They waited five more minutes for Kesh to finally come. He strolled into the basement as if he had no worries, and he walked with his head held high. His dreads were pulled back from his face, and he had changed into something more formidable. When Tiev saw him, his nose turned up instantly.

"So he arrives, finally!" Tiev started. "Only five minutes late, might I add."

"But I'm here." Kesh turned to the Sefu and offered their stale faces a smile. "As promised."

Tiev stood to one side and Kesh to the other. An elder vampire by the same of Solé stood between them and faced the audience. He was short, and the long hair on his head and chin were whiter than the whitest snow. He wore silver robes, and Risa couldn't help but think that he resembled something out of *Harry Potter*. His smooth skin barely had any wrinkles in it, and his voice boomed with a rasp in it that couldn't be missed.

"We are here to determine our true king. We are here to choose our leader!"

The crowd began clapping and cheering. Solé put his hands up to quiet them all down. When they calmed slightly, he began to speak again.

"We need a leader who we can trust, someone we can depend on in this world where we have nobody but each other. Someone who will not leave us in the time of need and someone we can depend on to fight for our honor! Whoever we choose as our leader, we will vow in blood to follow from now to eternity."

He paused and allowed the audience to clap. Risa felt her hands clapping too.

"What do you think is going to happen?" Cera whispered.

"Hopefully the right thing," Risa responded.

They waited for the crowd to get settled again and then Solé allowed Tiev to speak. Risa watched him step forward, sure of himself, ready to fill them all with even more lies.

"I was not the first king of this clan, but I am prepared to be the last. This last year was not easy by far, but I think we got through it like a breeze. We are still one, and if not as strong as a year ago, even stronger. I plan to keep the energy we have going flowing for eternity. I, unlike Kesh, will never leave any of you high and dry." He looked at Kesh and shook his head. "Believe me when I say that I would never want to take the place of my brother. I served beside him my whole reborn life, but I cannot sit back and let his path of destruction become ours."

The crowd began to clap, and Risa couldn't help but roll her eyes.

"Why aren't you cheering for your man?" Cera whispered sarcastically, and Risa cut her eyes at the young vampire.

"Kesh willingly brought a mortal into our home and, if that weren't enough, turned her into one of us. He replaced his vampire family with a makeshift one of his own. Not only that, but he brought a war to our front door and left us alone to fight it. If it were not for me, the Malum would still be down all of our throats! Lastly, he refuses to share with us the magic of having children. Is he the only one who deserves to be a father to a child who is biologically his? Should we all be forced to walk the path of not being able to reproduce? To conclude, he is a selfish vampire, not one I see fit to rule over us any longer."

Risa sucked her teeth and let her tongue linger on her right fang. Tiev had given a good argument and, by the looks of it, the rest of the vampires in the room thought so too. Risa hoped that Kesh had a good counterargument because, if not, things were not looking too good for him.

Solé motioned for Tiev to step back and for Kesh to step up. Kesh stood silent, allowing his head to swivel around the room. His eyes connected with each set of eyes staring back at him. They were expecting him to say why Tiev wasn't fit to be their king, but he would not give them the satisfaction. The only things he had to address were those that had to do with him.

"Sefu! I stand here in front of you as your estranged king. I take full responsibility for my actions, and I know you are all expecting an apology from me. And, unfortunately, it is an apology that I can't give."

The entire crowd burst out in a fit of boos and angry shouts. Risa's eyes were wide, and she wondered what the hell Kesh was thinking. If that was his idea of winning the clan over, he had another thing coming. Beside her, Cera was wearing the same confused expression.

"What is he doing?" Cera whispered.

"Give him time." Risa hid her worry. "Let him speak."

She and Kesh locked eyes, and she gave him an encouraging nod. When the shouts died down, Kesh placed his hands behind his back and continued.

"The reason I can't apologize is because if you sit here before me doubting me now, then you have always doubted me. I have done my job as your king seamlessly and, because of that, you are all stronger than you could ever imagine. If I have betrayed you, then your faith has betrayed me. If you truly believe that I would willingly leave you, my family, then you are wrong." He paused, and the entire room was so silent, one could hear a pin drop. "In order to keep my queen and my child safe, I had to leave. Sadly, I did not leave you in capable enough hands. As a clan, you should not be divided the way that you are. You have cliqued up like the college students you impersonate every day, and I fear that you have all forgotten the way of the Sefu. We are and have always been one. I am back to remind you of that."

"What about the child?" someone in the crowd shouted.

"The key to reproduction never was in me. Whoever told you that was lying," Kesh said. "Adirah Mesa, my queen, is the direct descendant of an Ancient vampire who was given the gift of life. That is how my son has come to be."

"Ancient vampire?" Tiev scoffed from behind him. "Preposterous! Everybody in this room knows that there is no such thing. Those are just stories, folktales!"

"Well, I can assure you that the folktales are very real," Kesh said. "I have seen them."

"Liar!"

"Tiev, you can say many things about me, but when have you ever known me to be a liar?" Tiev's mouth formed a straight line, and Kesh continued when he said nothing. "Sefu, the choice is yours. I know you will make the right decision."

Solé motioned for Kesh to step back when he was done speaking. Kesh didn't know if he was seeing things, but he could have sworn that the elder vampire smiled his way. He gazed into the sea of beautiful faces and took notice that their expressions were not as icy as they were when he first started talking. Some of them were giving him their nods of approval already.

"Now we vote!" Solé said. "It is time for us to choose the vampire we wish to follow until the end of time. We will do this simply: I will say the name, and you will raise your hands."

Risa watched Tiev. She fought the urge to slap the smug look from his face. If only the Sefu knew that he was a traitor among them. She uncloaked her mind and shot a thought directly at him.

Traitor.

Her distaste for her former lover had caused a glare in her eyes so powerful that when Tiev looked for the source of the thought, his eyes grew wider than she'd ever seen them. He realized that it was her voice he heard in his head; and, just so there was no confusion, Risa shared with him the conversation that she and Kesh had had in the hallway. She wanted Tiev to know that she knew everything, but mostly the fact that he was the one who betrayed the Sefu. Not Kesh.

"By a show of hands, who is in favor of Tiev as the new king of the Sefu clan?"

Risa's chest inflated with happiness as her insides smiled when she looked around and saw not a single hand in the air. Not one.

"By a show of hands, who is in favor of Kesh, king of the Sefu?"

Risa's hand flew to the sky along with Cera's. It was a unanimous decision. Every hand was up in the air, including Solé's. Kesh bowed his head to them and turned to Tiev. He shook his head as he looked at the sorry excuse for a vampire in front of him. When he spoke, he talked in only a voice that Tiev could hear.

"You were once my brother," he said. "I gave you nothing but loyalty, and in return, you tried to kill my family. But now you are my enemy and a traitor to his own clan. I will not punish you by death, but you are no longer welcome, and I renounce you from the Sefu. There will be many long nights, but if any of those long nights lead you back to this clan, I will not be so merciful next time. Leave, and take nothing with you."

Tiev thought about fighting Kesh right then and there, but with the Sefu choosing the side they were on, attacking him in front of them would not be very wise.

"Very well," Tiev said calmly: too calmly.

"Show him to the door, Solé," Kesh instructed. "We will have no more traitors among us."

Solé nodded and glared at Tiev before doing what he was told. Kesh waited for Solé to return before making another move. It took about five minutes, but when Solé returned, he gave his king a nod.

"He put up a fight, but he is gone."

"Good," Kesh told him.

While everyone was already gathered, Kesh figured there would be no better time to tell them the true reason of his return. His eyes fell on the seats that Cera and Risa had been in, but they were not in them anymore.

"Looking for us?" The voice belonged to Risa. She and Cera were both standing behind him facing the crowd of vampires. "We figured that you could use some backup with what you're about to lay on them all."

Their presence empowered him. They may have voted for him to remain their king, but would they follow him into war?

"Sefu!" Kesh grabbed their attention once more. "I came here tonight to regain your trust, but there is also another reason. Danger is near."

"Danger?" a few voices echoed.

"What kind of danger?"

"We have reason to believe that hunters are making their way here as we speak."

"Hunters?"

"How do you know this?"

"The Malum told me. They have a spy," Kesh said after a brief pause. As he expected, their response was deafening. "It is not what you think. The Malum are no longer our enemies! And their king has stepped down from his throne for me. Besides the hunters, there is an even greater danger that stalks us. It is time that vampires stop feuding with other vampires. Whether we like it or not, we are bound by race, and it is time that we act like it!"

On the last word, he opened up his mind to the room. Words would only do so much, and he knew it; they would need to see what he saw. He showed them everything that he'd learned and even gave them a glimpse of the Ancients' castle.

"Is that real?" Solé asked once Kesh blocked his mind from them again.

"Yes," Kesh said. "The more time we waste feuding, the less time we have to prepare for the

Ancient Lykan's return. I know I am not the only one in this room who feels its presence. We must get to the Ancients' castle and prepare for war."

"What about our home?"

That time, Cera answered. "We all knew that eventually we would have to leave this campus."

"Yes," Risa intervened. "This place has served us well, but now, especially since the hunters know where we are, we must go. The choice is yours."

"It is time that we leave this childish life behind us and become who we were all meant to be."

Cera and Risa shared a look before turning back to the crowd and saying in unison, "Warriors."

"We don't have much time. We have wasted most of what we had on this vote that you all just had to have."

"Risa," Kesh said.

"What? It is true. It is only hours until sunrise and—"

The sound of feet running down the stairs made Risa stop midsentence. The vampire named Aman was dressed as if he had just returned from a party, but there was no hint of fun anywhere on his face. He was in a state of panic and soon they would understand why.

"Hunters! Hunters are here!"

Chapter 22

The Sefu, skilled as they were, were caught off guard. The Malum spy had been wrong; the attack happened hours before sunrise, and there were more hunters than expected. They were war ready, and the ammunition that they brought with them let Kesh know that they didn't plan on letting any vampire leave alive. These hunters fought differently; Kesh took immediate notice of it. Not only were they wearing military gear, they were fast like vampires and even as strong.

"Do not be intimidated, Sefu!" Kesh called out as he launched a hunter to the side. "Do not let them into your home! This ends right here!"

"Aughh!"

Kesh heard the battle cry of one of the hunters coming his way, but the man was never able to get close. A hand through his chest made him stop in midstride, and he dropped when that same hand removed his still-beating heart. The hand belonged to Risa, and she dropped his heart next to his body.

"Not my king," she snarled.

"Thank you," Kesh said. "They are different."

"They have gotten stronger!"

Risa's face and hands were completely covered in the blood of the hunters she had defeated. She was a dangerous weapon and Kesh was happy to have her there with him. As soon as Aman made the announcement that the hunters were on their grounds, Kesh and Risa immediately went to meet them. She and Kesh fought side by side outside, not permitting the hunters access inside. The Sefu followed their leader into battle without a second thought.

"Their bullets—"

"Ultraviolet," Risa finished for him. "How are they moving so fast?"

"I don't know, but there are too many of them."

It had been a long time since Kesh had come in contact with a hunter. Moving the Sefu around so often helped, but eventually it was inevitable. The last time he had come face-to-face with one, they were still fighting with garlic and trying to get close enough to shove a stake through the heart. Their guns were so loud that the entire campus must have heard the fight that was ensuing.

Around him, all he heard were battle cries and the sounds of death: death of his people.

Ashes were everywhere, but so was blood. The entire front lawn was stained. The Sefu held their ground, not allowing the hunters access to the house, but how much more could they take? Kesh, fully transformed, let out a loud growl.

"Not my people!" he shouted. "Not my home! Ahhhh!"

A hunter tried to sneak up behind Risa with his automatic weapon aimed, but Kesh was too quick for him. He grabbed the gun by the nose and yanked it, causing it to fly into the face of another hunter. Kesh landed a power punch to the chest of the one in front of him and, when the hunter flew back, Kesh used his speed to catch him before he hit the ground. Kesh grabbed the hunter by his hair and forced his head to cock, giving Kesh the perfect view of his jugular vein.

"You want a savage beast? I will give you a savage beast!"

With that, Kesh bared his fangs and bit down on the hunter's neck, feeding until the man no longer moved. When he was done, Kesh threw him to the side like a rag doll and went on to the next. He fought brutally, with no regard for the lives of anyone but his own kind. He felt himself grow stronger with each hunter he fed from; and, by the time he stopped to look at the war zone, he'd already caught fifteen bodies.

Still, there were so many of them, and he felt like they just kept coming. Vampires were dying left and right around him. The Sefu would need a miracle if they hoped to survive.

His senses tingled, and he jumped high in the air to avoid being riddled with the bullets of an automatic weapon. They had come from the right of him, and when he looked, he saw that the shots had not come from just one gun. It seemed as though the hunters had targeted him as the deadliest, because there were five of them gunning for him.

"Kill their king! Aim and fire!"

Kesh had to move faster than he'd ever moved before. None of the bullets had a name on them so he raced to the back of the house so that none of the other Sefu would get hit. The hunters followed him, and they were fast, but not fast enough to see where he went.

Kesh was perched up on one of the gargoyles on the second story of the old frat house. The shadows were his best friend at that moment, and he used them to shield him. He watched the hunters creep into the back of the home, and he tried to read their minds. He got some images and pictures, but their thoughts were completely shielded, and he wondered how that could be.

"We lost him, sir," one of the men spoke into a walkie-talkie.

"No, we didn't," one of the other hunters said. "He's back here somewhere. He's watching us."

Kesh recognized the female voice. It was gruffer than he remembered, but there was no mistaking it. Lina. She was suited up like she'd been hunting for years. The way she held her gun, sure of herself, she seemed like a completely different person. Her eyes graced every inch of the back of the house, trying to find where Kesh was hiding.

"There!" she shouted, spotting him perched on the gargoyle.

Kesh moved just in time and evaded another set of bullets streaming his way. He leapt down from the gargoyle so fast that when he attacked the first hunter, his gun was still aimed at the place Kesh was previously. Using his claws, Kesh quickly slashed the throats of the three hunters with Lina. When they dropped, Lina tried to throw a punch at Kesh, but he caught her fist in midair, spinning her around. As he was pulling her to him, she attempted to get a shot off. Bad idea. Kesh dislocated her arm, forcing her to drop the gun with a cry of pain.

"You brought these people to my home," Kesh growled in her ear.

"You are all monsters," Lina panted and tried to stomach the pain shooting up her arm. "You all deserve to die."

"Even Adirah? Wasn't she your friend?"

His question caught her off guard. In all the time of planning and training, not once had the relationship that she had with Adirah crossed her mind. She thought of Narum often, but not so much of Adirah. But, at that moment, she felt nothing but loathing toward her former roommate. Maybe it was because she'd left her high and dry to become popular. Or maybe it was because Adirah had found true love. Now she too had a purpose, one that wasn't going to be changed because she used to be friends with somebody.

"She's a monster now too. Because of you. Whether it is I or somebody else who kills her, her blood will be on your hands."

"And your blood will be on mine."

It wasn't until the words were out of his mouth that Lina realized her mistake. Nobody spoke about his queen in such a way; Kesh wouldn't stand for it. He could have easily killed her right then and there, but he wanted her to feel pain. He gripped her by the hair and flung her high into the air. He went on to play a game of volleyball with himself and her body, beating her to a bloody pulp. He would not let her body touch the ground, so all she felt was the continuous pain coming from his power punches. When he was finally done with her, he let her drop ten feet to the ground. She was barely breathing and could not move a single muscle. Her eyes were swollen, and her jaw was cracked and at an odd angle.

"I should finish you off, but I want you to feel your death coming."

Kesh glared down at her for a second, but the sound of cheering through the gunfire in the front caught his attention. He could hear the battle still going on, and he suddenly was nervous. Maybe the hunters sent in another fleet. He ran to the front to see what was going on, and relief washed over him.

"The Malum are here!"

"They've come to help us!"

It was not the hunters he had heard cheering; it was the Sefu. And, sure enough, there was Talum, leading a group of Malum into battle on the huge front lawn. The hunters, who had had an advantage at first, were no match for both the Sefu and the Malum.

Kesh skimmed the crowd until he found who he was looking for. Adirah was in the middle of fighting two hunters at once. Calum was close by, and from the looks of it, they were handling themselves well. Kesh was about to take off in their direction when a voice stopped him.

"Kesh! King of Sefu!"

The voice was deep and gruff, but it got Kesh's attention. Whipping around, Kesh found the owner of the voice standing a yard away from him aiming a firearm at his chest. Kesh had never seen him before, but that moment the hunter's face was being etched into his memory forever.

"How does it feel to see your people dying around you, and you can't do anything about it but sit and watch?"

"People?" Kesh hissed. "I thought we were monsters to you."

"Such a smart-ass, aren't you?" The hunter chuckled.

"What is your name, hunter?"

"Ramel. Commander Ramel."

"Commander? So you are the one in charge here?"

"Obviously. However, I don't see how any of that matters now."

"It doesn't. I just wanted to know who you were before I ripped your throat out."

"You kill me? Funny, because I'm the one with the gun."

Boom!

The shot rang out before Kesh could react. There was a blur in the corner of Kesh's eye and right when the bullet should have connected with his chest, it didn't. But it hit something.

"No," Kesh said in disbelief. His eyes were wide, and he caught Cera as she clutched her chest. "Cera!"

"You were right. I have gotten faster," she said weakly, smiling sadly up at him.

"Why would you do that?"

"Because you are my king," she said as he cradled her. "You are the reason for everything. We need you, and for that, I give you my life."

"Cera," Kesh whispered, but it was too late. She had already begun to dissolve into ashes.

"Take care of our people. . . ."

Her voice lingered until Kesh was left holding nothing but air. There were tears in the corners of his eyes, and his body trembled from rage. He understood that, to many, they were monsters. But, in all actuality, there was no bigger monster than humankind. He clenched his eyes shut and gritted his teeth.

"Why do you torment my people? What is it that you want?"

"For you all to die."

"So that humans can become the superior race?"

"So that humans can be the only race!"

"That's never going to happen."

Kesh felt something inside of him awaken that he'd never felt before. It was like a door opened and released a force that had been locked away for so long. When he opened his eyes, they were no longer the same color brown; they glowed an electrifying blue. His fangs slowly grew longer, and his muscles grew so large that the robes he was wearing ripped. When he got back to his feet, he did not stand; the wind around him picked him up.

Ramel, not knowing what else to do, lifted his gun and began shooting at the new monster. Kesh looked nothing like any vampire he'd ever seen before. Not only were his eyes a shocking blue, but his skin seemed to glow more vibrant. Although the bullets were calculated and aimed directly at Kesh's body, the vampire dodged each one. Ramel reloaded and went to shoot again.

"Stop!"

Ramel froze, not because he wanted to, but because he didn't have a choice. He heard the word in his head and instantly his body was paralyzed. The only thing he had control over still was his eyes, and they watched Kesh move closer and closer to him. Once directly in front of him, Kesh grabbed Ramel by his neck and lifted him so that his feet dangled in the air.

What's happening? Ramel thought as he gasped for breath.

He was inside of his own head, but he didn't feel alone. Someone was going through his mind like they were flipping the pages of the most interesting book. He didn't understand. The concoction, it shouldn't have worn off yet.

"Ahhh. So that's what gives you hunters the strength and speed of our kind."

Get out of my head, Ramel demanded.

"But it's so fun in here!" Kesh's laugh echoed in Ramel's mind. *"I'm learning so much about the ways of you hunters. It's just ironic, isn't it? That your sole purpose is to remove the world of supernatural beings, but yet here you are using the potions of witches to do it. Tsk tsk tsk. But I guess, these days, everyone is a hypocrite."*

Fuck you!

"It looks like our good friend Lina already handled that for you."

Kesh brought forward the memory of Ramel and Lina having sex. It was still so fresh in Ramel's mind that every detail played. He had never felt more violated in his life, and his hatred for Kesh grew by the second. Little did he know, that same hatred was feeding Kesh's thirst.

Just kill me already!

"I will, eventually. Call your dogs off."

I—

"You can, and you will. Or else once you all are dead, what is left of us will go to where the

Legion for Darkness resides and pluck them limb from limb." Kesh pulled the location of the hunter's camp to the front of Ramel's mind, letting him know that the secret place wasn't so secret anymore. *"Call them off, and leave."*

The last statement was a command and Ramel couldn't fight it. When Kesh dropped him to the ground, his hand instantly shot to his neck as he coughed violently. Once he caught his breath, he pulled the walkie-talkie from his pants pocket and put it to his mouth.

"Retreat! There are too many of them. Retreat!"

"Good dog," Kesh said. "Now go!"

He kicked Ramel in the face so forcefully that he drew blood and Ramel flew back. He watched as hunters ran to his aid and helped him to his feet. From behind the frat house, Kesh saw a big man with a scar on his face carrying Lina's lifeless body as they all retreated.

The vampires were confused by the random retreat but were relieved nonetheless. Their eyes locked on their king and they noticed the difference in his appearance. His eyes . . . his eyes were like the ones they'd seen in the books about—

"Ancients," he heard someone in the crowd mutter.

Even Talum looked on in awe at Kesh. He was tired and panting, but he couldn't have been prouder of the way the Sefu and the Malum fought together. He walked fifty feet to stand in front of Kesh. Once there, he slowly took a knee and bowed his head.

"Kesh, king of all vampirekind."

Behind him, the two clans did the same thing. "Kesh, king of all vampires!" they shouted in unison.

Kesh's electrifying eyes found Adirah standing next to a kneeling Calum. She nodded once at him and placed a hand over her heart. He had done it, something that a year ago would not have been possible. He had united the Sefu and the Malum as one.

Chapter 23

"How badly is she hurt?"

"Pretty bad, Commander."

Ramel stood, looking at Lina's lifeless body through a glass window. She was on a table in the infirmary, unresponsive. Since they'd returned, he'd come to check on her every hour, but still, nothing changed.

"Will she survive?"

Doctor Ameel was doing everything in his power to keep Lina alive, but her heart rate kept dropping, and they kept having to resuscitate her. At the pace she was going, she wouldn't make it to the next sunrise, but that was the last thing that he wanted to tell Ramel.

He didn't have to say it, though. Ramel could tell by the grim look on the doctor's face. He banged his fist on the glass of the window before leaning his head on it with his eyes clenched shut. Lina's smile flashed in his head, and that was followed by the sound of her laughter. If only he hadn't been so pushy for her to be a hunter. Maybe she wasn't as ready as he thought she was.

"Don't give up on her," he whispered over his shoulder. "She isn't gone yet."

"Sir, I'm sorry. We have done everything that we are able to do. If she does not come back on her own, then I'm afraid there will be no bringing her back."

"That's not true. You haven't tried everything."

"I'm sorry? I'm not sure I quite understand what you are saying."

"You haven't tried everything. You know exactly what I'm saying."

"I do apologize, sir, but I am not at liberty to discuss that with someone of your rank."

"Then who is?"

"Commander." Dr. Ameel placed his hands in his white jacket and shook his head. "Even if you were to speak with them, or even get the okay to go forward with the procedure, there is no telling if it would work. Every other test patient has died."

"Has it ever been tested on a human?" When Dr. Ameel didn't say anything, Ramel faced him. "I didn't think so. Who do I need to talk to?"

"Commander, you don't know what you're asking. She is not awake. You would have to make the decision for her. Is this something that she would want?"

"She would want to live."

"She wouldn't be human anymore."

"And she wouldn't be one of them, either."

"Commander," Dr. Ameel said, sighing, "the studies we have run on vampire blood are still under much scrutiny. We don't exactly know what the outcome would be. We don't know how they heal, or if they too will be immortal."

"All I keep hearing you say is what you don't know. How about you tell me what you do know?"

"I know that the animals we injected with the vampire blood grew very savage, at first. They, however, did not exhibit the thirst for blood the way vampires do. It was obvious, though, that we had awakened a different kind of beast in every creature. They were stronger, smarter, faster. And—"

"And what?"

"Uncontrollable."

"What are you saying?" Ramel's brow furrowed. "That the vampire blood wasn't what killed them?"

"Precisely. The last animal we tested was a gorilla to start with. Her name was Ella, very shy and timid. Once she was injected with the vampire blood, she became a remarkable subject.

She had the most promise of them all but, after a while, it became almost impossible to contain her. She killed three scientists in a brutal rage. We had no choice but to put her down."

"Has it ever crossed your mind that the reason why the testing has not worked is because you are injecting animals that have no sense of humanity? You can't base what might happen to Lina off of what those animals have done. Tell me something: without the procedure, how much time do you think she has left?"

"Maybe—"

"Maybe what, Doc?"

"Maybe a day or two. Give or take."

"Then I don't really have another choice, do I? And I'm not going through anyone higher than me to save her. You are going to get me what I need and bring it back here."

"I could be fired."

"Or you could be dead." Ramel touched the gun on his waist. "You take your pick."

Dr. Ameel pressed his teeth together hard until a vein popped from his temple. He glanced from Lina's emotionless figure and back to Ramel's undaunted face. There was something underneath his hard expression that Dr. Ameel knew all too well.

"Do you love this woman?"

"What?"

"Do you love her?"

"Why does that matter?"

"Because once she is changed, it is going to take a special kind of person to remind her of who she is. It is going to take something strong to bring her back from the monstrous virus we are injecting into her system. It will take love for her to get over the curse you are placing on her. Do you understand that?"

"Yes. But there is no other way. I can't . . . I can't lose her. She's special."

"Then meet me here at three a.m. That is when the last scientist leaves the lab, and I will be able to get what we need. Oh"—Dr. Ameel had started to walk away, but he paused to turn back to him—"you might want to bring that special serum of yours. Because when she wakes up, trust me when I say she will be wide awake."

"Just make sure you're here right after."

"I will. And, Commander?"

"Yeah, Doc?"

"Good luck."

Chapter 24

Snarls and saliva became the air as two Lykans dueled in a large cage. Mezza looked down from his seat and watched them lay into each other like their lives depended on it, which they did. They were all in a building separate from his gigantic mansion; they were in the war chamber. That was where, since his beginning, Lykans trained. Mezza wanted only the strongest of the strong in his army. The crowd of hundreds around the cage were loud, and many of them were standing in their seats, rooting for who they wanted to win. Mezza, on the other hand, was quiet. The two large beasts were both adamant about winning, that was for sure. Mezza could tell that those two beasts had been around for a while. No matter what damage was caused, they would not give up or bow down.

When, finally, he tired of the vicious fight, he put his hand up and motioned for the guard in the cage to separate the two monsters. As they were pulled away from each other, they transformed back into their human bodies and collapsed in the corners, gasping for air.

"Your chests heave like that of someone who has just fought a victorious battle. I am pleased by the way you fight." Mezza nodded at the cage. At the sound of his voice, everyone grew quiet and turned their heads to face him. "You are relentless, and you don't give up. We will need that, for I sense that the vampires are growing stronger."

He stood and stepped into the aisle of stairs so that he could come down them. As he passed, each of the surrounding Lykans felt his powerful aura. He was growing stronger by the day.

"Ahhh, yes." He smiled evilly. "You feel it, don't you? That, my children, is the strength that comes with the nearing of the full moon. This time around, you will be faster."

The Lykans cheered loudly.

"Stronger!"

More cheering.

"And smarter! On the night that we attack our enemies, our oppressors, you will all take a drop of my blood."

He had reached the ground, and he spun to face them with his arms up. They were all on their feet by then, baring their sharp human teeth and flexing their abnormally large muscles. Mezza had empowered them and given them meaning they never knew they had. Before coming to his home, they were all miscreants. But, with the upcoming war, Mezza had given them purpose, informed them about the truth of their nature, and embedded entitlement in their minds.

"The world calls us beasts! Are we beasts?"

"No!" The shout that came back to him was deafening, and Mezza loved it.

"That's right! We do the same thing as every other living being on this planet: we survive! If they want to kill us, then we will slaughter them first! We will slaughter them until they are no more! We will pick away at the races that have shunned us since the beginning of time and show them that we are and have always been more than rabid dogs! What are we?"

"Superior!"

"Superior!" Mezza repeated in a shout. "And we will show the world!"

He turned his back on them and made his way to the exit of the building. Even when he was out of the building and walking on the trail that led to the mansion, he could still hear them cheering behind him. He gritted his teeth as he thought about his brother, still in slumber. He did not know where he lay resting; he also didn't know why he hadn't awoken yet. There was only one way to find out that answer, because there was only one person who knew.

"Dena." He growled her name under his breath.

She was the one who battled and weakened Tidas. It was she who finally bound him down long enough to use the witches' powerful magic on him. Wherever his brother was, she would know.

Since he'd been awakened, he had searched for the Ancient vampires' secret fortress. He figured that the place was heavily warded by witches' magic, but he never thought it would be impossible to find. The Lykans were so worked up about the upcoming war, but if Mezza did not locate the fortress in one week's time, all of their training would be for nothing. Although strong, Mezza was no match for the Ancient vampires alone if he did not have the power of the full moon.

He was so lost in his own thoughts that when Cairo approached him, he snatched the young Lykan up by his neck. "Do not sneak up on me like that," Mezza stated once he saw who he had in his clutches. He released Cairo but did not apologize. "What is it that you want? Why aren't you in there training with the others?"

"They never let me fight with them." Cairo looked away. "They tell me I am weak."

"Are you?"

"No." Cairo looked Mezza in the eyes. "I am as strong as any Lykan here. Well, besides you, of course."

"Why haven't you told them that?"

"Because I would rather show them. I have come to ask if you would train me personally, sire. I want to be an asset to the war."

Mezza studied the determined look on Cairo's face and wondered how many days it took for him to muster up the courage to ask his question. Cairo was the only Lykan there who dared to address Mezza directly or even to invade his personal space. He didn't know how he felt about it exactly, but at that moment it did not make him uneasy. In fact, he remembered being a young Lykan like Cairo. Had it not been for Tidas, he would have never found his way.

"Walk with me," Mezza said and continued on the path.

"Yes, sire." Cairo did as he was told.

They walked in silence for a short while before Cairo realized they should have been at the mansion a long time ago. He looked behind him and saw that they'd passed the mansion and had been walking in a circle.

"It's crazy, isn't it? The things that transpire when you are lost in your own thoughts. That's the third time we have passed the entrance, and you are just now taking notice of it. Tell me, young Lykan, what is on your mind?"

"I was just thinking."

"About?"

"You, sire. I was wondering what it would be like to be in a slumber for centuries and waking up to this world."

For the first time since he'd been awake, Mezza found himself chuckling. Mostly because he remembered opening his eyes in a clearing, naked, and not knowing where he was. The first thing he felt was the hunger. The centuries and centuries' worth of hunger. He ripped apart every animal he saw and was so full by the time he spotted his first human he did not even have the urge to eat her heart. Nor did he want to chase after her when she screamed seeing all the blood that stained his face and clothes. Things had changed drastically since he was turned.

Everything was different. The humans dressed and spoke differently. When he learned of the year, 2017, he almost dropped where he stood. He'd been in slumber for almost one hundred years. As he slept, the world had gone on without him. All the havoc he and his brothers had wreaked was all for nothing. They were forgotten, almost as if they never existed.

"You would think that after all those years of sleep, one would wake up with a new objective. Maybe have an entirely new outlook on life."

"You don't?"

"No." Mezza stared in front of him at nothing in particular. "I woke up with the same thirst I had the day my brother and I were put to rest.

Though I am in a new era, it feels as if just yesterday I fought the Ancient vampires. The rage I felt then still is caged inside of me and battling to escape. I will not be at peace until they are all dead and I awaken my brother."

"Where is he?" Cairo asked and suddenly wondered if he'd overstepped his boundaries.

Mezza's face grew dark at Cairo's question, and he paused in his stride. His hands clenched and turned into fists and his eyes flashed like there was fire in them. It only lasted a second, but in that second Cairo pondered running the other way. When Mezza's face returned to normal, he sighed and shook his head.

"I don't know," Mezza confessed.

"Who does? The Ancient vamps?"

"Yes."

"Then we will kill all of them until they tell us."

"First we need to locate their fortress. And we need to find it before the full moon." Mezza sighed.

He did not understand why he was telling the young Lykan his woes, but he was. He looked over at Cairo's face and wondered if that was how he looked when he was under Tidas's wing. The other Lykans ganged up on him for his size but, once, Mezza had been small like him too. Tidas told him that a fight was never about the size of the body; it all came down to the size of the heart. All Cairo needed was a little direction and he could be the greatest general known to all Lykans. He definitely had the drive.

"Have you ever heard the story of how we Ancients were created?"

"No." Cairo shook his head but then corrected himself. "I mean, I've heard stories, but I doubt they were the right ones."

"Enlighten me."

"Well, one of them says you were all bitten by wolves when you were fresh out of the womb."

"Interesting."

"And another says that you were all stranded for a year in the woods as children and you came across . . ." He stopped talking, seeing the amused expression spread across Mezza's face.

When Mezza noticed that Cairo had stopped he urged him to continue. "Continue. I want to hear this."

"As much as I would like to entertain you with my stories, I wish to be granted knowledge, sire. It is obvious that I am wrong. How did you become Ancients?"

If Cairo had been anyone else, Mezza might have ripped his tongue out for responding to him in such a way. Cairo, however, got a pass. Mezza placed his arms behind his back and held his head up high. The memories flashed through his mind like a horror flick. He heard the screams and saw all of the blood as if the scenes were happening right before his eyes.

The pain that used to squeeze his heart now felt like only a pinch.

"There was once a time when I could not think about it. I didn't want to. But, as I grew into my powers, I realized that what had taken place was now a part of me."

"What happened?"

"I could tell you." Mezza turned so suddenly to face Cairo that he jumped. He placed two fingers on Cairo's forehead and began to share a vision. "But I'd much rather show you."

"Tidas! Catch!"

Sixteen-year-old Mezza ran barefoot on the dirt and grass along with his older brother. They were a little ways away from their people in northeastern Africa, and they wore nothing but a pair of woven shorts. They were known as the Krag, a tribe that their father, Soldaat, was the chief of. His two sons, Mezza and nineteen-year-old Tidas, often liked to adventure off, but he encouraged it. One day, Tidas would need to lead his people. It was important for them both to know every inch of what surrounded their home.

Whereas Mezza had lighter brown skin, Tidas was as dark as a blackberry. He was handsome in the face and wore his hair woven in one braid on the top of his head. He had straight white teeth and deep dimples on both cheeks. His brown eyes were lighter than his skin and always looked to be filled with laughter. In both of his ears, just like Mezza, he had two thick golden hoops, signifying that they were the sons of the chief.

"Got it!" Tidas shouted as he jumped high into the air and caught the disc that his brother had thrown his way. "You are getting better, little brother."

"My arms are getting stronger!" Mezza slapped one arm, and then the other, before flexing them both.

Tidas laughed and threw the disc back. When Mezza caught it, Tidas jogged to where he was and patted him on the back. "How is training coming?"

Mezza's shoulders slumped slightly, and if Tidas didn't know his brother the way he did, he would have missed it. Mezza looked on to the setting sun and remained silent. Tidas didn't like the vibe he was getting, and he placed a comforting hand on his brother's bare shoulder.

"Mezza, is something wrong?"

"It's Leeu. He's hard on me," Mezza said, speaking about his father's general.

"He is supposed to be. He is training you for battle," Tidas said, but Mezza shook his head.

"No, he's harder on me than on the other boys. I think he hates me."

Tidas sighed. He knew why Leeu treated him in such a way, but he was restricted from ever telling Mezza the truth. To Mezza's knowledge, he and Tidas had both the same mother and father. If he were to know that their mother, Reën, was not his biological mother, there was no telling what he would do. Soldaat's infidelity was known to none but Tidas, Reën, and Leeu.

Leeu once had a daughter named Asha. At the time she was the same age that Tidas was now, next to Reën she was the most beautiful girl in the tribe. Every man had his eyes on her, including the chief. Her pregnancy shamed Leeu so, but when it came to light that the father was none other than Chief Soldaat, he had no choice but to hide the pregnancy. Asha was all he had left in the world after his wife passed, and when Asha died in childbirth, he was left alone.

Chief Soldaat banned him from ever telling Mezza that he was his biological grandfather and he went on the raise the boy himself. Reën, although angry with her husband for disobeying their vows, grew to love Mezza as much as she did Tidas. If Tidas had to guess, Leeu's anger with Mezza was not because he hated him. It was because he loved him and could never express it the way he should have been able to.

Tidas sighed. "He doesn't hate you."

"How do you know?"

"Because I'm your big brother, and do you think I would let someone who hated you train you hours of the day?"

Mezza smacked his lips. "You are always so busy with Father that I doubt you would even notice."

"Brother." Tidas gripped Mezza's arms and forced his baby brother to look into his eyes. In them, he saw sadness. "I would give my last breath before I let someone cause you harm. There are some things that you just wouldn't understand, but just know that everything is not what it seems."

"Whatever," Mezza said. "All the other boys get time to learn, but with me, I'm expected to know everything because I am the son of the chief. He beats me with sticks if I do something wrong. I never get the chance to do it right. How am I supposed to learn like that?"

"If it makes you feel any better, I can train you at night."

"But won't you be tired?"

It was true that Soldaat had Tidas training like crazy as well, but he did much less combat those days. Soldaat mostly taught Tidas about the ways of their people and how to survive the harshest of conditions. He missed the one-on-one battles with his peers. It had gotten to the point where no one could defeat him, but he still enjoyed the rush that came with the fight.

"Never too tired for you, Mezza." Tidas shuffled his hand on Mezza's head. *"I would be no use to you if I did not teach you to be my equal. After all, if something happens to me, this tribe will be all yours."*

"Well, I pray nothing happens to you." Mezza shook his head. *"I was not born to lead."*

Tidas grinned, but his next statement was cut short by a bloodcurdling scream in the distance.

"It came from the village!" Tidas said, alarmed. *"Come on. We may be under attack."*

Not another second was wasted. The boys ran full speed in the direction of their village and were alarmed at what they saw. The Krag were all in disarray as they ran frantically around, calling the names of their loved ones. The smoke caught Mezza's attention, and the fire caught Tidas's. Their homes were being destroyed before their very eyes, and all of their warriors lay slain in the middle of the village. Mezza ran to where they were and looked down into the faces of every boy his age in his class. Dead. They were all dead.

"Their chests." Mezza's eyes were as big as the disc in his hands. *"Their hearts are gone."*

"Father! Mother! Nooo!"

Mezza ran to where he heard his brother shout. He was in the chief's hut, and Mezza braced himself for what he was about to see. The entrance was smeared with blood, and his breath quickened as he entered. His first sight was their lifeless feet, and then their bodies. They were sprawled out on the ground at awkward angles, and Tidas kneeled at their sides. Mezza couldn't remove his eyes from his mother's once-beautiful face. She was unrecognizable. Something had mauled her to the point where her nose wasn't even attached anymore.

"What has happened?" Tidas's voice shook. "Who has dishonored our parents in such a way?"

Mezza couldn't stand the sight anymore. He backed out of the hut and went back outside, although what he saw there was not any better.

"It's coming!"

"Run!"

"My baby! It killed my baby!"

"Where is my son?"

"Mommy! Mommy!"

Chaos was all around him. He spun in a circle, trying to find the creator of it all, but he saw nothing but fire and mayhem. In the midst of the frenzy, he heard the faint sound of someone choking. Scanning the bodies, he finally found the source of the sound. It was Leeu. He was gripping his stomach, and Mezza could see there was a big chunk of his trainer's side missing.

"Leeu!" Mezza ran to the elder man and knelt beside him. "Who did this?"

Leeu's mouth moved as if he was trying to say something, but nothing came out but a gurgle of blood. He used his free hand to grab Mezza's arm and pull him down. Mezza understood what Leeu wanted him to do and he put his ear close to the man's mouth.

"What is it, Leeu? Who did this?"

"W . . . witches!"

"What?"

"The beast!"

Mezza did not understand what Leeu was trying to say, but his guess was that being so close to death was making him mad. On his face, Mezza felt Leeu take his last breath, and his hand released Mezza's arm. He went to sit back up, but before he was all the way upright, he felt himself be tackled to the ground.

"Watch out, brother!"

He and Tidas rolled on the dirt, and Mezza cut his arm on a sharp rock. He didn't need to ask why Tidas had tackled him, because when they stood, he saw exactly why. A wolf as big as three was crouched down and baring its teeth at them. Its muzzle looked as if it should have been white, but the thick red blood that covered it made it impossible to tell. Tidas looked around and found two spears from the slain warriors near his feet.

"Mezza," he said and handed his brother the second spear. "Do not be afraid."

Tidas crouched down as well and swayed, trying to anticipate the wolf's next move. Mezza did the same. He took slow steps to the right, putting space between himself and his brother. It would be harder to attack both of them if they were not in the same spot. The wolf kept his eyes on Tidas, snarling at him.

When the beast attacked, both Mezza and Tidas assumed it would go for Tidas. But the creature was smart; it had faked them out. His eyes had been on Tidas, but the whole time he'd been focusing on Mezza. When it leaped, Mezza's senses kicked in, and he sidestepped out of the way. He used the back end of his spear to forcefully knock the wolf's head to the side. He tried to jump back, but the wolf recuperated too quickly. Its claw slashed and sliced the skin on Mezza's chest.

"Ahhh!" Mezza shouted in pain, but he did not back down.

The large wolf pounced on Mezza's small body, and the only thing that kept its snapping mouth from chewing a hole in Mezza's face was the wooden spear being held on his neck.

"Brother!"

But he didn't even need to call for his help; Tidas was right there. Without another second passing, Tidas shoved his spear into the wolf's *right temple, killing it on impact. The heavy beast collapsed on Mezza's body, knocked the wind completely out of him.*

"Hold on, little brother," Tidas said and used all of his strength to push the dead weight off of Mezza. "There."

"Tidas," Mezza panted. "The village."

"We must go and aid our people."

"But the village—"

"The village is no more! We have to go. Before more of these unnatural things come."

Not too far away, the boys heard the sound of hands clapping together. Although their energy was depleted, they jumped to their feet and assumed their battle positions at the sight of the woman before them. She was unlike any they had ever seen, and she was dressed in black cloaks. In her hair, she had matted braids, and the wrinkles under her eyes gave her young face an old look. Although it was a hot day, the closer she got to them the colder their insides got.

"He's right; this village is done for." Her edgy voice echoed in the air. "And so are your people."

She waved a hand in the air, and the few members of the tribe still scrambling around suddenly dropped to the ground clutching their necks. They tried to gasp for air, but it was like they were suffocating.

"Who are you? What are you doing to them?" Tidas asked in horror. When she didn't answer, he shouted again. "What are you doing to them?"

The woman cackled but still did not say a word. She twisted her hand, that time causing the choking people to rise from the ground. Their feet flailed wildly, and their eyes were wide, not understanding what was going on. When their eyes began to bulge out of their sockets, Mezza could not stand it any longer.

"Put them down!"

"As you wish." The woman smiled sinisterly, revealing black teeth, and she flicked her wrist once more. The people dropped five feet to the ground, dead. "Happy now?"

"Why have you done this to my people? What did we do to deserve this slaughter?"

"Nothing. My pet was just hungry." She cackled again before her expression grew sinister once more. "You killed him."

"It tried to kill us first."

"He!" the woman corrected him. "Tatu was a loyal protector, my only friend. And you will pay for every drop of his blood that has leaked on the ground."

"No," Tidas sneered. "An eye for an eye. Tatu killed my parents."

"Do you think I care about the lives of a few mortals? No! I care about myself and that I will not be forced to walk alone and unprotected. You two? Yesss, you two will be my new protectors. Drink!"

Mezza panicked when he realized he no longer had control of his own body. Both he and Tidas took heavy steps toward where the dead wolf lay. Mezza tried to fight against the force that had overcome him, but the more he fought, the more pain shot through his limbs.

"Witch!"

"That's what they call me." She cackled again. "I prefer my name, Aika: a name that you will be very familiar with! Now drink!"

She waved her hands and forced them to get on all fours. As their faces neared the corpse of the dead wolf, they heard her saying an incantation in another language. Before their eyes, the pool of red blood turned golden right before they took their first drink.

Mezza released Cairo, and the boy took a step back, gasping for air. He tried to make sense of the vision that Mezza had shown him and couldn't help but feel pity for his king.

"Your entire family—"

"Slaughtered, like cattle. All because the witch and her pet were bored."

"So you were created by witches?"

"Yes."

"What about the others? I thought there were five of you."

"Yes. They were created by Aika in the same manner."

"You worked for her?"

"Yes, for many years. She and other witches used us as guard dogs. That is, until—"

"Until what?"

"Until the pain and sorrow of what they had done to us became too much to bear. Our lives were stripped from us, and we were turned into beasts that they should have never expected to control forever. Aika did not know it then, but she had made us much stronger than she intended. We had the mixture of mortal, wolf, and witch magic dancing around in our DNA. We were unstoppable."

"Until the creation of the first vampires."

"Yes, the witches' second set of pets. Their favorites."

Cairo noticed the resentment dripping from his tone. "Where are the witches now? In hiding?"

"No, they never hide. They're watching, as they always do. And now that I am awake I am going to give them the show of their miserable, lengthy lives. Once we have defeated the vampires, we will then go after the witches' coven."

Cairo gulped. After Mezza had shown him the image of Aika, he hadn't been able to get it out of his head. The last thing he wanted was to face an army full of women who looked like her, but he would follow Mezza into any battlefield. Suddenly he remembered the other reason why he had approached Mezza.

"Sire! I have news," Cairo said. "I should have said this first, but then we got to talking, and you showed me the vision and—"

"Cairo, slow down and speak."

"Sorry, sire. Our human spy has told us that the vampires have begun to move out."

"Where are they going?"

"I'm not sure, but from the sounds of it there are hundreds of them."

Cairo's words were like music to Mezza's ears, and he might never know it. Mezza's handsome human face spread into an animalistic smile and his forehead crinkled.

"I knew that they would sense my presence. Send trackers to follow them at once," he said. "Make sure they keep their distance and are sure to not be seen. The vampires are headed to to Ancients' fortress to prepare for the full moon.

Cairo, we will soon know the location of the Ancient vampires."

His sinister laugh filled the air and caused the birds to take off from the trees that they were perched in. He finally found the missing piece to his puzzle.

To Be Continued